喚醒你的英文語感！

Get a Feel for English !

喚醒你的英文語感！

Get a Feel for English !

同步解決TOEIC考題

解決洋問題的英語力

內附 MP3

作者— 陳超明・蕭婉珍

✓租屋 ✓協商交涉 ✓簽約 ✓交通問路 ✓銀行開戶
✓點餐打包 ✓購物退換貨 ✓郵寄包裹 ✓申辦手機…
帶你輕鬆迎戰海外生活中的各種疑難雜症！

貝塔語言出版
Beta Multimedia Publishing

我在美國唸書的時候，外國老師的授課方式跟台灣不太一樣。他們喜歡拋出很多問題，給很多課前閱讀，藉此訓練學生獨立思考、腦力激盪，自己去找尋答案，任務導向的學習方式幾乎隨處可見，學生可以從完成任務中學會應有的技能。今日台灣雖慢慢走向這種模式，但大部分的課程仍舊是給予學習者最終答案，讓學習者記住後再去應用。因此學習者熟知問尺寸要說 "Do you have this in size 8?"，問價錢要說 "How much is it?"，但真的讓他自己進入店內購買，他又怕得不敢行動。

近幾年出國的人數愈來愈多，不論是留遊學，或是現在正夯的度假打工。但是即便這些人都已具備了一定程度的語言能力，他們仍舊很惶恐，為什麼？因為使用語言達成基本溝通和使用語言生活，其實還是兩個概念。許多旅遊會話語句即使他們都可以應答無礙，但要由頭至尾獨力完成各項生活任務，他們卻不見得有能力應付。再者，雖說網路資源豐富，大家有事沒事就求助 Google 大神，可是零散資訊一堆，該如何抉擇取捨、整合應用，卻往往抓不著頭緒，結果英文用得四不像。

本書所設計的狀況都是我在國外唸書時實際遇到的問題，是語言問題，也是生活問題。我一直認為學習語言的目的，不應只是為了結交朋友、為了出國旅遊、為了完成一場完美簡報，而是應該要能確實將語言帶入生活、用於生活，作為輔助生活的一項利器。所謂的英文能力，不應只是會聽說讀寫，而是要學會整合聽說讀寫，幫助自己達成各項任務。本書期許協助學習者在平時就儲備好解決任務的能力，以日常生活中常見的食衣住行情境為主軸，進而發展延伸。不再只是制式的告知，而是引導學習者親自走入各情境，接觸到各項問題，一個步驟一個步驟真切地自己去思考、去應用。

接下來，請把自己當成 Carrie，邁入這趟充滿挑戰的旅程，你一定也能培養出解決問題的英語力！

蕭婉珍

CONTENTS

Chapter Outline

★☆ Situation & Work Schedule

於每章開頭之處列出該章的情境與學習重點，使讀者預先對即將學習的內容有概略的了解，並方便讀者在遇到問題時透過本頁即可找到相關對應章節。

🔍 Task

本書特色為以「任務」導向學習，將在美國生活有可能遇到的各種問題，敘述成一項項任務，帶領讀者跟著書中主角 Carrie 一起完成過程，並從中找到讀者自身欲尋找的解決方式。

✏️ Exercise

除了閱讀各種任務之外，本書更鼓勵讀者實際動手練習，以期收到真正內化為自身英語力之成效，因此作者亦精心設計多種練習題，包括填空題、連連看、聽力測驗（對話）、閱讀測驗等不同題型，讓讀者能夠不枯燥地「邊玩邊學」。

🔑 Key Words/Expressions

為了給讀者在腦力激盪時一些提示，特別將關鍵字詞彙整成表，一目了然。不僅可作為該章任務的解答之鑰，亦可適用於其他相同情境；只要記住關鍵字詞，在聆聽老外談話或閱讀英文文章時就能快速理解。

📑 Vocabulary Exercise

字彙力是眾多英語能力的基礎，故在此編排了有趣的 crossword puzzle 幫助讀者在輕鬆的氛圍下加強字彙認知，即使跳脫該章內容單獨做此練習也毫不乏味。

Summary

讀者不用擔心在本書的眾多實用資訊中迷路,只須查看此環節便能迅速掌握該章
所有學習重點,並可當作複習彙整使用,讓學會的英語力具體呈現。

TOEIC Test

由於多益成績是許多國人無論畢業或就職、升遷之際的關鍵,也是許多人報考的
重要英語認證測驗,而其實本書所介紹的眾多英語力皆與多益生活類試題密不可
分,因此在每章最後特別仿實測標準,各編寫一題聽力題或閱讀題,讓讀者同時
增強應試本領。

✂ 各章節內的對話、短文和 TOEIC Test 的翻譯收錄於書末,如有需要方便讀者
自行剪下對照使用。

本書使用說明

1️⃣ Task 和 Exercise 的答案為不影響練習成效，大多列於該頁置底或次頁最下方；少數情況由於編排緣故，則列於再下一頁，並於題目處標示清楚。

2️⃣ 本書所引用之網站資訊或頁面擷圖，由於網站不定期更新，正確資訊請以最新公布資料為準。

3️⃣ 關於 Key Words/Expressions 與內容之對照方式：

• 在對話當中：

> **Operator:** Hi, T-Mobile. How may I help you? ──────────● **Key Expressions**
>
> **Carrie:** Hi. I'd like to sign up for a phone plan for my cell phone.
>
> **Operator:** No problem. What plan would you like to get?
>
> **Carrie:** Actually, I've checked your website, and am very interested in your
> (1) _____. But I'm not sure if I need to sign a contract.
>
> **Operator:** All the phone plans in T-Mobile have no (2) _____ service contracts
> any more.
>
> **Carrie:** Sweet! And what about the overage fees? I read that I can use up to 2GB of 4G
> LTE data. How much do I need to pay if I go over that limit?
>
> **Operator:** No domestic (3) _____ will be charged. That means if you go over your
> allocated amount of data, you can still use it, but at a reduced data speed. So ──────────● **Key Words**
> besides associated taxes and surcharges, $50 will be all you have to pay.

• 在其他內容裡：

> **Checking account:** A checking account offers easy access to your money for your daily ──────────● **Key Words**
> transactional needs and helps keep your cash secure. Customers can use a debit card or
> checks to make purchases or pay bills. Accounts may have different options or packages
> to help waive certain monthly service fees.
>
> **Savings account:** A savings account allows you to accumulate interest on funds you've
> saved for future needs. Interest rates can be compounded on a daily, weekly, monthly, or
> annual basis. Savings accounts vary by monthly service fees, interest rates, method used
> to calculate interest, and minimum opening deposit.

4️⃣ 關於 CD 光碟

收錄全書所有對話與聽力測驗內容，由外籍專業配音員錄製，發音準確、自然生動。時間約 24 分鐘，容量約 33 MB，為 MP3 格式。

 導論

★☆ 將英語當成第一或第二語言

把英語當外語來學習 (learning English as a foreign language) 的人愈來愈少。

未來英語學習的趨勢：把英語當成 the first language 和 a second language 的國家或人才會愈來愈多！

外語？或第二語言？到底有何不同？

把英語當成外語，很多人只是在學校學英語，把它當成一種知識或學科來學。過去，我們在學校都是這樣學英語的！

把英語當成第一語言 (the first language) 或第二語言 (a second language) 來學，代表的是使用英語作為溝通工具，而非當成學科來學。但是這不代表英語要講得多好，而是能達到使用英語溝通的目的。

例如新加坡人的英語其實沒有想像中那麼好，他們說英語的速度很快，而且能溝通，大多數人以此為生活與工作的溝通工具；很多人家中的菲傭英語也沒有很好，很多單字、文法都會講錯，但是他們可以用英語和人溝通。對他們而言，英語就是第二語言 (a second language)。

雖然台灣許多人的發音、文法、閱讀能力都比菲傭好很多，可是我們卻把英語當成 a foreign language 的學科來學，溝通能力自然會比不上把英語當成 a second language 來學的菲傭們。

★☆ 將英語當作國際溝通語

現在，我們應該把英語視為 international language（國際語言）。

首先我們要認清溝通的目的。最重要的是表達語意，而非講得跟母語人士一樣，亦即我們的英語不必像英美的母語人士 (native speaker) 一樣好。

以我自身為例，唸到博士之後到大學教書，我深深感覺到再怎麼努力，我的口說英語還是不如美國小學生道地。我講英語會有口音 (accent)，對美國比較細微的東西或是一些生活知識、事務可能不了解，也不懂美國的兒歌或是一些遊戲的玩法。值得深思的是，我們的英語是不是需要像美國人一樣好？

其實是不需要的。英語最重要的是其功能性，我們學習英語的重點是要有能力完成所須完成的工作，也就是我們要學習全球人士使用的英語：全球英語 (Global English)。

★☆ 什麼是全球英語（Global English）？

第一位提及此全球英語概念的是法國退休的 IBM 執行長 Jean-Paul Nerriere。他認為英語在二十一世紀已經成為第三千禧年的世界方言 (The worldwide dialect of the third millennium)，是一種國際語言，已經不帶英美文化的臍帶與原始影響。它已經成為一種全球意識 (Global Consciousness)，具有傳染性、調適性、民粹性與顛覆性。所謂傳染性指的是英語已無形中漸漸成為大家共同的溝通語言；調適性指的是此語言會因地方、文化的發展，而從英美式的英語成為區域性或排除文化性的一種共同語言；所謂民粹性指的是，它已經不是知識份子或精英份子的標誌，而是庶民都可以使用的一種工具；顛覆性則提出其打破正統、傳統或典雅的英語規範。這種語言簡單地說，就是一種簡化版、去英美文化色彩的大眾英語！

★☆ 區域多樣性讓母語人士失去英語的專利權

全球已經超過十多億人口將英語當成第二語言，這些人口超越了原來將英語當成第一語言的英美人士。英語的掌控權不再屬於英國人或美國人。

身為英語非母語者，應該要具備能夠以英語來溝通、解決問題的能力，而毋須達到如母語人士般沒有口音的目標。台灣人每次看到老外，經常會以 "My English is very poor." 來當開場白，我覺得英語非母語者在說英語的時候絕對不需要道歉，就好像西方人絕對不會因為中文說得不好而向他人道歉一樣。

先前曾有國內的官員在外交場合上說："My English is very poor."（我的英語很糟糕），但與他對話的那名老外卻回答："No, your English is better than my Chinese."（不，你的英語比我的中文好），因為就老外的角度而言，他們會想我們到美國還要講英語，而他們來台灣仍以英語溝通，所以沒理由要道歉，反而是他們不會說中文才應該感到不好意思。

★☆ 語言學習方式的改變

全球英語的發展，到底對英語學習有什麼樣的改變。首先，英語不單單屬於母語人士，其次，英美文化的學習並非是必然的。其實最重要的是，學習英語的目標改變：英語被當成一種實用工具 (English as a practical tool)。

全世界有三種語言學習的模式，第一種是東北亞模式，把英語當成外語來學，語言一開始學習，首先把基本一萬多個單字及文法學完後，才開始溝通。身處東北亞的我們學不好英語就是因為把它當成學科來學，認為須學好結構後才能做練習或實用。

另外一種是東南亞模式，即從街頭英語 (Street English) 學起，也就是先用，錯了再糾正。例如泰國曼谷小攤販的英語看似很好，事實上他們也只會幾種英語用法，但他們講的英語都是有功能性的，對他們而言，運用這些英語就足夠他們生活。

台灣人可能要學會第一人稱、第二人稱及第三人稱的 be 動詞變化後，才能說：I am happy; you are happy; he is happy; everyone is happy; we are all happy.。而東南亞很多小孩子都不用這些——I happy; you happy; he happy; everyone happy; we all happy.，那些複雜的 be 動詞變化全免了，但表達的語意還是很清楚。

當然，東南亞模式有其缺點，它的學習可能是偏 low level 的範圍。我認為最好的語言學習模式是歐盟模式，歐洲國家英語最好的是德國，德國人的英語從兩個來源學習，第一是學習語法，第二是學習真正實用的英語。因此，他們把英語當成日常生活用語，也就是學習得到且用得到的英語，用不到的則不學。德國人從語用的概念來學英語，不把它當成學科，所以英語才會學得好。

新的學習方法：情境學習（Situated Learning）的理論說明

美國語言學家 Jean Lave 曾提到情境學習是種有效且持續的語言學習方式，這種她所謂的「合法性的邊緣性參與」(legitimate peripheral participation)，認為有效學習是情境式的，是跟活動、情景、文化所結合的。這是一種非刻意式 (unintentional) 的學習方式。

例如我把英語小說當成一種娛樂消遣，而非學習英語的方法。我每天放鬆自己享受書本所帶來的樂趣，不知不覺把許多英語深深刻印在腦裡，完全不費吹灰之力。這是一種將學習融入生活的過程，就像小孩子學說中文不是在學習說中文而只是在生活、成長。就好比許多一句英語都不會的老年人知道巷口的便利商店叫做 SEVEN-ELEVEN、兒子買咖啡的地方是 Starbucks 一樣，因為這是每天在聽、在接觸的東西就能夠不經意地講出來。就像我們天天聽捷運上的英語，久而久之就深刻在腦中。

Legitimate Peripheral Participation 指的就是，學生能夠透過社會互動及合作 (social interaction and collaboration) 來更有效地學習，也就是透過「做事」或參與活動，來進行語言學習，這就是情境學習的關鍵。

★☆ 如何使用英語？

我們便必須思考一個很重要的問題，那就是如何在無英語環境之下創造英語使用的機會？台灣人對於英語學習的迷思就在於強調此語言的學習 "learning" 而非使用 "use"。若我們不使用英語那為什麼要學習它？知道一個單字跟會使用一個單字是兩回事，我們真正要做的是 "doing" 而不只是 "knowing"。舉個例子來說好了，學游泳時從書本上瀏覽再多相關知識、熟記再多划水技巧都不夠，重要的是要實際下水去游，這種實際到真實的場景中學習的方式正是我所要提倡的情境學習法。

早期的語言情境學習方式強調結構性，提供學習者大量的句型來記憶並且培養以語言情境回應的能力。例如我們常看到的餐廳場景或問路場景，列出數個句型讓學生去套用，但問題就出在學生若是遇到課本中沒有涵蓋的練習範圍，便會措手不及、不知如何反應。直到目前為止，市面上大部分的教材都還在使用這種陳舊的錯誤學習法。

現在的情境語言學習強調的是一種社會文化學習法。這是一種文化性且非刻意式的學習，強調單字與文法的功能性以及聽說讀寫四大技巧的融合。透過解決問題的過程，使得學習涵蓋了知識性與內容性、合作性與互動性、動機性與合理性。

★☆ 從工作及案例中學英語：解決問題

我在一些政府及私人訓練單位教授英語的時候，拋棄了強調舊式聽說讀寫的方式，採取分配工作事項的策略，設計不同的 cases、tasks 給學生，比如說老闆要出國參加會議，身為助理必須要安排一切並解決其中可能碰到的問題，在完成 case 的過程中可能會碰到的接機、轉機、艙級升等、行李遺失、飯店安排等問題便大量地涵蓋了英語聽說讀寫的機會，這也是我所強調的 problem solving 能力。

透過這種真正使用英語的學習方式，才會令學習者印象深刻，不需要刻意去背、去記憶，即所謂情境學習 (situated learning) 的概念。在不知不覺中透過工作，把真正有機會用到的英語學起來。這種順便學起來的學習方法，也就是上述所提及的非刻意式的 (unintentional) 學習方法，才是真正有效的學習方法。

由此看來，我們該顛覆以考試為主的學習，轉而運用情境學習，這種真正有效的方法來增進自己的英語能力。準備坊間的能力測驗，如多益考試也是如此，多益考題大致上分十種情境，從真實生活 (real life) 擷取設計成題目，所以我們要做的就是把題目還原成真實生活去使用 (use)，不用背、不須記憶便可輕鬆上手。

★☆ 透過社會運作習得英語：社會文化理論

此外，俄國心理學家 Vygotsky 在其提出的社會文化理論中 (Social Cultural Theory [SCT]) 表示當一個人在學習第二語言時，文字不僅「表示不同的物體和動作，還能夠將學習者對語音的生物理解轉變為對文化和概念的理解」。因此，在談論語言如何幫助溝通時，了解文字的文化意涵與引申意義是比了解文法架構更為重要的觀念。

他認為，要培養出這種溝通能力，必須要有一套社會文化的語言課程。內化 (internalization) 就是習得這種能力的一環。要將語言內化，首先要會模仿。但是模仿並非指不經思考單純的模仿，而是包括了「有目標的認知、能夠重新塑造原本的認知」(Lantolf and Throme 203)。當學習一個外國語的基礎（單字或句型）時，學習者必須要觀察該語言眞實生活的溝通方式。要成功學會一個語言，就是要結合文法學習與了解社會情境。

這也就是我想強調的「只要了解就不須記憶」的語言學習法。我認爲，學習語言跟智力或記憶力完全無關，大部分歐洲人都會講三種語言，但他們的智力並沒有比我們高，任何智力較低或不足的人還是能學會他的母語，這就是所謂社會情境的力量。由此看來，我們一直以來都把語言學習的重心放錯地方了。

語言學習應該考慮與認知學習的關係 (cognitive apprenticeship)，這是一種在某種知識領域 (domain activity) 中學習，引導學生在眞實情境活動中獲得並發展認知工具的學科與知識互動的方法 (co-produce knowledge through activities)。學習可以在教室內與教室外，透過合作性的社會互動 (collaborative social interaction) 與知識的社會建構 (social construction of knowledge)，如透過文化認知了解語言使用、透過活動與社會互動來產生眞實的練習。

★☆ 解決問題的英語力：實施情境學習的最好方法

實行這種眞實練習最好的方法就是透過解決問題的過程。這種透過解決問題 (problem solving) 來培養能力的方法，相對於學校練習 (school activity)，提供了我們眞實練習 (authentic activity) 的機會。舊式的學校練習強調 knowing（知道），透過解決問題來學習的方式則提供了 doing（動手做）的機會，而這兩者是環環相扣且密不可分的。我們要知道學校所教的跟眞實情況的差別，把兩者結合才是重點。

因此，我們應該開始重視學生培養解決問題的能力，修正學習重心。如同近來政府的十二年國教也開始推動小學生要有解決問題的能力，而這也正是我們這本書的重點：透過解決問題來學習全球英語！

★☆ 如何評量自己的英語，是否符合全球英語的能力？

現在我們對非母語人士要求的英語能力，是要有批判性思考和解決問題的能力，而不是著重在有沒有 accent，如前所述，我的英語或許沒講得比美國小學生好，但是我的英語能力卻不會比美國人弱，因爲我可以用英語思考及解決問題。區域多樣性讓母語人士失去英語的專利權，有時候口音已變成區分文化的一種媒介。

如果我們要強調英語已變成國際語言，我們可能要知道母語人士在使用英語時會碰到問題。反之，母語人士可能要重新學全球英語。如果母語人士要講英語的時候，應該要學最常用的 1500 個單字，我們可能不太會去注重一些諺語或片語，例如我們會以 make efforts 取代 pull out all the stops，可能不會用 obtain 而是用 get 這個單字，未來的語言學習，我們可能是用 Global English 的方式來學習的。

★☆ 學習英語的目的為何？

至於要學到何等地步？那就要先自問學習英語的原因為何？問自己是否會想跟英語為母語者溝通？是否想在國際場合中與外國人商談？或是在國際場合中表達自己的觀點？又或者是想教英語？還是單純是為了在國外生存而學英語？或是想出國旅行？要先決定學習英語的目的是什麼，再決定需要學哪方面的英語，以及要達到怎樣的程度。

★☆ 以情境式的方法學習語言

在學習英語時，可以透過目標管理的概念進行。假設學生在畢業後只想在石門水庫旁開間咖啡廳，還是需要具備基本的英語能力。因為咖啡豆可能要從國外進口，當有外國觀光客光顧時，也須以英語溝通。此時，不用去讀所謂的英語操作手冊，而是要學相關領域的英語及一般日常生活用語。

除此之外，也需要思考什麼場合會用到英語，是買東西時？還是職場上？其次要思考的是為什麼要學英語？需要透過什麼方式才能有效學習？

最後是要思考，自己要再加強哪部分的能力？單字？文法？溝通技巧？口筆譯？批判性思考？又或者是解決問題的能力？台灣目前的學習仍著重在語意學習，較缺少批判性思考和解決問題的能力，但是在職場上卻比較需要後者的能力。

★☆ 多益是種情境：解決問題就是多益考題！

情境學習不是去製造一個情境出來，而是在一個情境之下，學習語言的互動性以及將之內化變成自己的語言。像是多益、全民英檢、IELTS 或是托福都可以用此方式學習，托福的考試方式是到美國的二十所大學錄製上課情境，之後做摘要把它當作考試的題材；多益考試則是蒐集商業公司間的 Email 或是一些公告，把實用性和生活性的題材整理出來，依照情境進行配題。多益不是考英語，而是考如何用英語來解決問題，所以它具備批判性思考和解決問題能力。這才是現在職場會用到的東西，而不是去背好幾萬個單字。

現在台灣很強調一個問題，到底英語是要具備正確 (accuracy) 還是流暢 (fluency)？也就是說正確性是否有像想像中那樣重要？

我個人認為，如果沒有影響語意的文法就不是那麼重要，像是 "a" apple 跟 "an" apple 都一樣是蘋果，錯了也不會影響意思，也不會從蘋果變成柳丁。如果我們今天要在國際場合與他人競爭的話，就需要學習 Global English。至於如何學習和學些什麼？從 speaking 和 writing 反推，最重要的是要有產出 (production) 的能力。要講、會寫，也就是除了要會聽，也要看得懂。換言之，從目的性倒過來到語言上的溝通，最重要的是：把英語當作國際溝通的一種工具。

　　我們在校園裡或在職場上，都會遇到大大小小的問題，這些使我們產生焦慮。問題該如何解決？

　　其中最大的困難，來自於完成工作過程中不預期的狀況與困境。現況與想要達到的預期目標之間，如果產生差異，就是所謂問題產生。例如，你們公司本來邀請一位德國客戶來台灣洽談訂單、參訪工廠，一切你都安排好了。然而，星期一卻碰到颱風，該德國客戶滯留香港，所有行程延遲！此時該怎麼辦？

　　具備解決問題的能力，成了生活或職場上必備技能。因此，最終為了要達到預期目標，我們必須找出許多方式來應對、來解決問題！

★☆ 解決問題的步驟

　　以英語來說，要解決問題的過程有數個步驟：

■ 找出問題 identify the problem

　　任何問題一發生，首先要先找出問題的癥結在哪？不少人對過程不夠清楚，對於目標也不明確，所以間接用錯了釐清癥結的方式。

　　找出問題癥結有下列幾個有效方法：

■ 跟別人比較一下	comparison with others
■ 找出一些弱勢的地方	monitor for weak signals
■ 跟目標或過去的表現做些比較	comparison of current performance with objectives or past performance
■ 列出工作清單	checklists
■ 腦力激盪	brainstorming
■ 列出抱怨	listing complaints
■ 角色扮演	role playing

就前述德國客戶的例子而言，問題在於如何調整行程、如何安排後續的後勤支援。除了比較之前的做法外，也可列出可能的工作清單，最後腦力激盪，找出一些真正的問題。

二 探索問題 explore the problem

在解決問題前，我們必須釐清這份工作是從何而來、由何人所交代、為何會產生此工作、又是何時產生的？詢問諸如此類的 who, what, when, where, and how 的問題，並且將之詳細列出，便能有效地幫助接下來找出問題的解決方法。

三 設定目標 set goals

在這點中，最重要的是：填補問題及目標之間的縫隙 (fixing the gap between the problem and the goal)。現在的問題跟未來想達到的目標有何差距，找出想達成的目標，自然可以找到彌補差距的方法。

四 尋找解決的方法 look at alternatives

尋找有效的解決方法有數個步驟：

■ 分析過去的解決方法	■ 提出問題
■ 閱讀	■ 討論
■ 資料蒐集	■ 用不同角度檢視問題
■ 思考	■ 腦力激盪

我們要設法盡可能地列出能夠解決的方法，以便接下來的決策動作。

五 將想出來的解決方法 (alternatives)，做 mind mapping（心智圖）

把 issue 放在中間，所有方法擺在旁邊圍繞著，清楚地畫出整體概念。

接下來的步驟就是用消去法 (a slow process of elimination) 找出最好的解決方法，並考量情況 (circumstances) 及資源 (resources)，例如人、金錢、時間、步驟、政策、規定等是否都能符合。

六 執行 implementation

首先最重要的是溝通，因此英文口語表達在這點就相當重要，如何清楚表達自己的意思，成了關鍵要素。

七 評估 evaluation

檢查所找出的解決方法夠不夠好。此時若能做一個 checklist 就很適合。此步驟是為了要檢視方法有無效果、過程合不合適或有無運用到最好的資源。

整理：解決問題的重要項目

由此來看，有效的問題解決方法有幾個重要的項目：

- 對問題清楚地描述
- 將有限的或負面的元素呈現出來
- 將建設性的或正面的元素呈現出來
- 釐清是誰的問題、何人能解決
- 釐清問題的範圍
- 設想問題無法解決的後果為何
- 將腦力激盪出的解決方法做出列表

★☆ 解決問題，創意很重要

我認為解決方法必須有創意：之前，曾聽過一個日本解決問題的故事，很有創意！

這是發生在日本一間照相館的事：一對到義大利遊玩的夫婦，回國後將底片送去此照相館沖洗。由於新手技術上的失誤，導致整捲底片的資料都被消除。在這個危機當刻，照相館主人決定自掏腰包，再將這對夫妻免費送出國旅遊一次。

這個消息傳遍日本，全國上上下下都在讚嘆這位相館主人的創意做法及誠懇服務態度，電視廣播也都在談論這個新聞，這位老闆巧妙地將危機化作轉機，不只主客盡歡，還免費得到了大打廣告的好機會。

這種極具創意的解決方法，不只有效，還能帶來額外收穫。另外一個例子則是來自現在最熱門的蘋果電腦。在美國，有一位丈夫將他新買的 iPad 2 退回蘋果公司，退回的包裹中有張紙條說明著退貨原因是：“Wife says NO!”。幾天後這位丈夫收到蘋果寄來包裹，一打開來發現那台他退回去的 iPad 2 送回來了，還有一張寫著 “Apple says YES!” 的紙條。同樣地，全世界的媒體爭相報導這則新聞，網路上也不斷討論蘋果的創意解決方法，除了完全擄獲這位丈夫的心，不但將他變成百分百的蘋果迷，也得到了在全世界免費廣告的大好機會。

★☆ 從語言觀點來看解決問題的能力

在前面提到的解決問題過程中，必須充分運用英語聽說讀寫四大能力。比方說一開始解決問題，事前準備過程如分析過去解決方法、閱讀或資料蒐集等都可大量訓練閱讀能力；在列出問題、解決方法清單等，都可訓練寫作；最後再藉由溝通、討論等尋找解決方法，以及最後執行甚至評估步驟，都大量運用英語聽力與口說練習，如開會報告或與對方交涉等。

上述為解決問題的基本流程，相信大家都會問：這與語言學習有何關聯？在本書中我們將會體驗到在解決問題的過程中不論是思考、閱讀或討論、執行解決問題的行為中，都必定要透過語言 (language) 來完成。透過語言溝通完成的過程中，英語便不知不覺地學起來了。我們不是強記一些單字或文法、句型，而是英語主動地植入我們學習者腦中，進而深深地烙印下來！

★☆ 邀請你一起來解決問題，強化多益考試能力

因此，本書以提供 task 的概念設計各方面可能會出現的問題，尤其是一般學生或社會人士必須面對的生活問題。此外，我們也配合多益題型，從理解廣告、租屋、購物、訂約等情境，來進行語言實作。從 task 中，掌握全球英語（多益英語）必須知道的單字與表達方式，利用聽力訓練、口語、情境閱讀、問題解決等實際操作，提供學習者一個嶄新的英語學習方式，不會忘記、不用強記。

讓我們跟隨本書主人翁 Carrie 一起前進美國，開始她一連串的英語情境學習，也幫她解決一切的生活與學習問題。

　　期望讀者的英語能力大躍進！

實踐大學講座教授
政治大學英文系兼任教授
台灣全球化教育推廣協會理事長

陳超明

Chapter 1

Collecting Information
蒐集資訊

在本章，你將會學習到如何蒐集資訊。

Situation: House Hunting 找房子

在大學畢業之後，Carrie 決定給自己一段時間，獨自前往美國遊學。不同於以往選擇學校住宿，這次她想要找尋一間套房自己一人住，但她卻不知道該怎麼著手進行。

☆ 你能陪她一塊完成這些過程嗎？

Work Schedule

☑ Look for Useful Information 搜尋有用資訊
☑ Locate the Information You Need 辨識所需資訊

TASK 1 Look for Useful Information

Online House Hunting 線上找房子

找房子除了直接透過房仲，也可在報紙上搜尋租屋的分類廣告。但時至今日，多數人喜歡利用線上房仲網 (online real estate) 來幫忙。不僅可以縮小居住範圍、填入租屋需求，還能即時在網上瀏覽物件的圖片，省去不少時間。

Step 1

要 Google 尋找線上房仲網一點都不難，連結到下面網站瞧瞧吧！
It's easy to Google many useful real estate websites online. Browse the website below.

<Website> http://losangeles.craigslist.org/hhh/

美國較大型的幾個租屋網站：

craigslist (http://geo.craigslist.org/iso/ca/on)

Kijiji (http://kijiji.ca/)

GSC Rentals (http://www.gscrentals.com/)

MLS (http://www.mls.ca/)

Ontario Student Housing (http://www.ontariostudenthousing.com/)

Step 2

雖然確認了區域所在：Los Angeles，但是在 "housing" 下還有一堆分類選項，哪些是 Carrie 可以考慮的呢？（答案自由發揮）

Selecting Los Angeles, Carrie finds a lot of options under "housing." Which ones can she take into consideration?

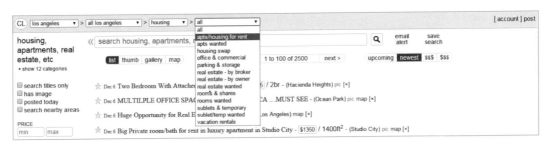

Exercise 1

下列選項哪些是給一般長期租屋者看的呢？（下表翻譯在第214頁）

1. apts/housing for rent	6. real estate – by owner	10. rooms wanted
2. apts wanted	7. real estate – by broker	11. sublets & temporary
3. housing swap	8. real estate wanted	12. sublet/temp wanted
4. office & commercial	9. rooms & shares	13. vacation rentals
5. parking & storage		

Answer

1. 公寓 / 房屋出租   9. 房間分租

Step 3

回到 Carrie 的需求，她要找的是間公寓。請幫她縮小尋找範圍吧！

Back to Carrie's requirement. She is looking for an apartment. Can you help her narrow down the choices?

Answer

apts/housing for rent（房東張貼頁面）

Step 4

縮小了範圍，而搜尋結果頁上的這些名詞是什麼意思？你知道多少公寓型式？（答案自由發揮）

So now, we've helped Carrie narrow down the choices. But what are all those terms on the results page? How many apartment types do you know?

✎ Exercise 2   🎧 Track 01

請聽 Carrie 和 Paul 的對話，並於空格內填入適當的詞語。（答案在第28頁）

■ lofts   ■ studio   ■ one-bedroom apartment   ■ two-bedroom
■ loft apartment ■ studio apartment ■ penthouse apartment   ■ three-bedroom

Paul: Hey Carrie, what's up? I heard that you're going to study abroad. So how's everything? Have you applied for the dorm?

Carrie: No, I have another plan. You know, I've been living in the dorm for the past four years. This time, I really want to live alone.

Paul: OK. Then how's your house hunting going? Have you found anything you like?

Carrie: Um ... no actually. I'm still working on the apartment types. Those posters use different names for the house, which really confuses me.

Paul: Don't worry. I think I can help you with that.

Carrie: Great! So where to start? Let's see ... (scroll down the page) OK. What's a (1) _____?

Paul: A (2) _____? Oh it's basically a small apartment with bedroom, living room and kitchenette all in one room plus a full bathroom separately. Some people call it an efficiency apartment or a bachelor apartment too.

Carrie: What about a (3) _____? I also see there are (4) _____, or (5) _____ ones.

Paul: Well, similar to a studio, a one-bedroom apartment also has a living room, a kitchen, a full bathroom but an independent bedroom, so you could have more privacy if you have friends visiting.

Carrie: Then I guess a two-bedroom apartment should have two independent bedrooms, right?

Paul: You got it! Sometimes, it comes with one more bathroom.

Carrie: Uh, I think I'm getting on track now. Good, so next are (6) _____.

Paul: A (7) _____ refers to large open space featuring high ceilings and without interior walls. The upper story is often the area for sleeping.

Carrie: Clear. Here comes the last one – a (8) _____ .

Paul: Wow, that's something you can hardly <u>afford</u>. A (9) _____ is a specially designed apartment on the top floor of a building. It's usually regarded as <u>luxury real estate</u> with everything inside, and surely very expensive.

Carrie: Relax. Of course I won't pick that one.

🔑 Key Expressions

> 🔑 **What's up? = How's it going? = How are you doing? = How are you?**
> 是很常見的問候語！
>
> 🔑 **How's (something) going?** 詢問（某事）進行得如何
> 例如問人工作如何就可以說：How's your job going?
>
> 🔑 **work on (something)** 從事（某事）、努力於（某事）
>
> 🔑 **You got it! = You're right!** 在這表示對方答對，了解了。
>
> 🔑 **come with** 伴隨著……
> 點餐時也常聽到，例如：
> All sandwiches come with salad or soup.（所有三明治均附沙拉或湯。）
>
> 🔑 **Clear.** 表示清楚、了解，單一個字就可以了。

🔑 Key Words

Word	Meaning
house hunting (*n. phr.*)	looking for houses 找房子
kitchenette (*n.*)	small kitchen 小廚房
separately (*adv.*)	apart from each other 分開地；個別地
independent (*a.*)	free from other's control 獨立的
privacy (*n.*)	space away from the public 隱私
feature (*v.*)	to have special mark of 以……為特色
ceiling (*n.*)	top surface of a room 天花板
story (*n.*)	floor, level 樓層
afford (*v.*)	to be able to pay 負擔得起
luxury (*n.*)	something very expensive 奢侈品
real estate (*n.*)	land or buildings you own 房地產；不動產

Idiom	Meaning
get on track	to start understanding something 進入狀況

請再聽一遍音檔，然後將下列房型填入對應的定義和圖片吧！

- studio apartment (efficiency apartment / bachelor apartment)
- full bathroom
- loft
- 1 or 2 bedroom apartment
- penthouse apartment

1 an apartment with a living room, a kitchen, a full bathroom and one/two independent bedroom(s) 一房或二房的公寓，含分隔的廚房、客廳、飯廳及衛浴

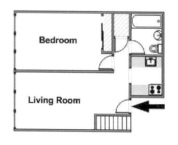

Ans._____

2 a small apartment with bedroom, living room and kitchenette all in one room plus a full bathroom separately 開放式套房

APPROX. 475 S.F.

Ans._____

Answer Exercise 2

(1) studio apartment   (2) studio   (3) one-bedroom apartment   (4) two-bedroom

(5) three-bedroom   (6) lofts   (7) loft apartment   (8) penthouse apartment

(9) penthouse apartment

3 a specially designed apartment on the top floor of a building, usually regarded as luxury real estate with everything inside 頂樓豪華公寓

Ans. _____

4 a large open space featuring high ceilings and without interior walls. The upper story is often used for sleeping 樓中樓或挑高兩層

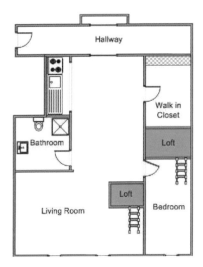

Ans. _____

5 a bathroom with a toilet, a sink, a bathtub, and a shower 全套衛浴

Ans. _____

(cf.) half bathroom
a bathroom with only a toilet and a sink

Answer Exercise 3

1 1 or 2 bedroom apartment   2 studio apartment   3 penthouse apartment

4 loft   5 full bathroom

根據張貼的標題，Carrie 接著要點選進去看看廣告內容了。除了圖片，Carrie 可以從裡面的文字敘述中獲得什麼資訊呢？

$1490.00 per month – RESORT STYLE LIVING IN A PRIME TOLUCA LAKE NEIGHBORHOOD (MOVE IN SPECIAL 1month free)

Contact Information

Andy
ad74ny@gmail.com
2121234789

Pricing

Rent: $1490.00 per month
Available Date: Sun May 15, 2016
Deposit: 500
Minimum Lease: 1 year
Included Utilities: water / trash

Property Location

4319 W Hood Ave Burbank,
CA 91505 VIEW MAP

Features

Bedrooms: 1   Bathrooms: 1
Located on Floor #: 1   Floors in Bldg: 2
Parking Spaces: 1   Pets Allowed: Cats & Dogs
Year Built: 1998

Attributes

RENTAL UNIT AMENITIES
• Refrigerator   • Dishwasher
• Hardwood Floors   • Stainless Steal Appliances
BUILDING AMENITIES
• On-site Laundry   • On-site Manager
• Swimming Pool   • Security Gate
OTHER AMENITIES
• Additional Storage   • Hardwood Floors
• BBQ Area   • Great Restaurants and Shops

✎ Exercise 1

根據上面的廣告，你可以猜出它們的意思嗎？試著連連看吧！（答案在第34頁）

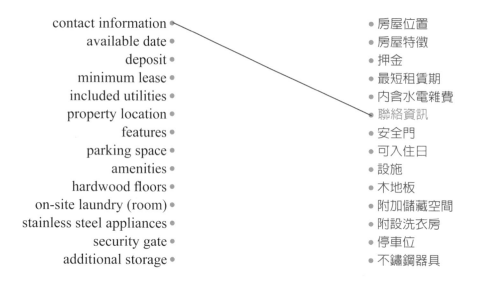

contact information ●   ● 房屋位置
available date ●   ● 房屋特徵
deposit ●   ● 押金
minimum lease ●   ● 最短租賃期
included utilities ●   ● 內含水電雜費
property location ●   ● 聯絡資訊
features ●   ● 安全門
parking space ●   ● 可入住日
amenities ●   ● 設施
hardwood floors ●   ● 木地板
on-site laundry (room) ●   ● 附加儲藏空間
stainless steel appliances ●   ● 附設洗衣房
security gate ●   ● 停車位
additional storage ●   ● 不鏽鋼器具

✏️ Exercise 2

還有什麼設備／設施是你會需要的呢？試著將下面幾種設備／設施填入正確的位置吧！（答案在第34頁）

- cable-ready
- air-conditioning (a/c)
- heater
- balcony
- walk-in closet
- microwave
- tile floor
- stove
- washing machine + dryer
- wireless internet (Wi-Fi)

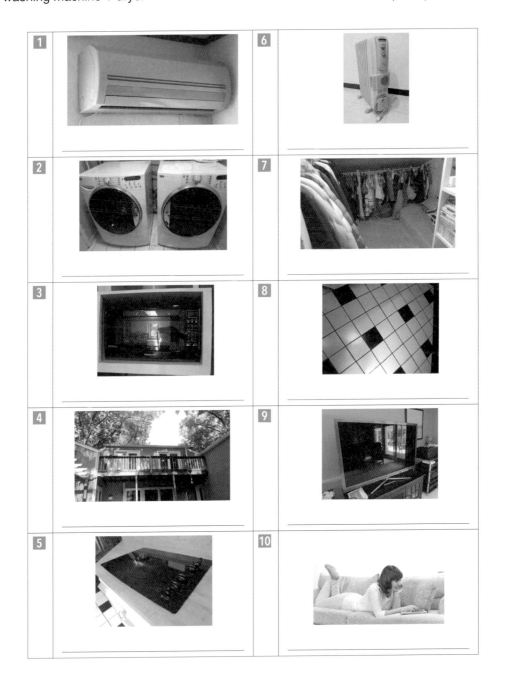

 **Exercise 3**

請閱讀以下短篇廣告。（翻譯在第215頁）

Posted: 2016-01-11, 3:13PM

$2,000 / 2br - SPACIOUS 2BED/2BATH APT - QUICK MOVE-IN (N. Vermont Ave, Hollywood, CA 90033)

Discover luxury living at Pleasant Apartment Homes. Pleasant offers spacious and cozy two-story apartments with 2 bedrooms, 2 full bath units, a/c & heating, a large walk-in closet, a private balcony, and four modern on-site laundry rooms open 24 hours. Assigned parking and garages are also available.

With a short drive to shopping, entertainment, dinning and close to downtown Los Angeles, Pleasant is conveniently located near the 66 and 5 freeways. Available now, 1 year lease, $2,000 per month, and $1,500 deposit required.

Come tour these amazing apartments. Our helpful and friendly on-site staff is ready to answer all your questions. We are open 7 days a week for your convenience.

根據上篇短文，請試著補上缺少的資訊。（答案在第34頁）

PRICING

Rent: $ (1)_____ per month

Available Date: (2)_____

Deposit: $ (3)_____

Minimum Lease: (4)_____ year

PROPERTY LOCATION

(5)_____ Ave, (6)_____, CA 90033

FEATURES

Bedrooms: (7)_____   Full Bathrooms: (8)_____

Floors in *Bldg (building): (9)_____

Parking Spaces: (10)_____

RENTAL UNIT AMENITIES

(11)_____ & heating

Walk-in (12)_____

Private (13)_____

BUILDING AMENITIES

On-site Laundry Rooms: Yes / No (14)

NEIGHBORHOOD

Nearby: shops, theaters, restaurants, downtown LA

Freeway Close

Word	Meaning	Word	Meaning
contact information	聯絡資訊	parking space	停車位
available date	可入住日	amenities	設施
deposit	押金	hardwood floors	木地板
minimum lease	最短租賃期	on-site laundry	附設洗衣房
included utilities	內含水電雜費	stainless steel appliances	不鏽鋼器具
property location	房屋位置	security gate	安全門
features	房屋特徵	additional storage	附加儲藏空間

Answer Exercise 2

1 air-conditioning (a/c) 冷氣機
2 washing machine + dryer 洗烘衣機
3 microwave 微波爐
4 balcony 陽台
5 stove 爐具

6 heater 暖氣機
7 walk-in closet 人可進出的大型衣櫥
8 tile floor 磁磚地板
9 cable-ready 有線電視
10 wireless internet (Wi-Fi) 無限網路

Answer Exercise 3

(1) 2000
(2) 2016/06/11 or anytime
(3) 1500
(4) 1
(5) N. Vermont

(6) Hollywood
(7) 2
(8) 2
(9) 2
(10) Assigned parking and garages

(11) a/c (air-conditioning)
(12) closet
(13) balcony
(14) Yes

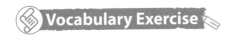

Task 1 Crossword Puzzle 填字遊戲

請根據下列英文提示，將該單字填入空格中。Hint: 可參考前面的 Key Words 表。

Down:

1. land or buildings you own
2. looking for houses
3. apart from each other
4. space away from the public
5. to have special mark of

Across:

6. free from other's control
7. to be able to pay
8. floor, level
9. something very expensive
10. top surface of a room

Answer

1. real estate	2. house hunting	3. separately	4. privacy	5. feature
6. independent	7. afford	8. story	9. luxury	10. ceiling

Task 2　Scrambled Words 字母重組

請將左方亂序的字母重組成有意義的單字。

1 HEEISHGDNEIRPTNTE　　　＿＿＿＿ ＿＿＿＿＿ ＿＿＿＿＿＿＿

2 IAOITNNIRNCDOIG　　　＿＿＿ ＿＿＿＿＿＿＿＿＿＿＿

3 GSINHEWNACHAIM　　　＿＿＿＿＿＿＿ ＿＿＿＿＿＿＿

4 IESNCLAWTLKO　　　＿＿＿＿ ＿＿ ＿＿＿＿＿＿

5 BCALRAYEDE　　　＿＿＿＿＿ ＿＿＿＿＿

6 LIETOFROL　　　＿＿＿＿ ＿＿＿＿＿

7 OAMCERWVI　　　＿＿＿＿＿＿＿＿＿

8 AYLCBNO　　　＿＿＿＿＿＿＿

9 EAHTRE　　　＿＿＿＿＿＿

10 EYRDR　　　＿＿＿＿＿

11 OEVTS　　　＿＿＿＿＿

12 NVOE　　　＿＿＿＿

Google some famous real estate websites and then click on them.
搜尋線上著名房仲網，然後進入網站。

↓

Narrow down your requirement to "apartment."
縮小搜尋範圍，找尋「公寓」。

※ 若是你已經有金額預算或是希望的房間數，也可在這時趕緊放入條件！

↓

Look for listings that fit your needs. 查看符合你需要的列表。

 房型常見的選擇有：
① **Studio Apartments** 開放式套房
② **1 or 2 bedroom-Apartments** 一房或二房的公寓
③ **Lofts** 樓中樓或挑高兩層
④ **Penthouse Apartments** 頂樓豪華公寓

↓

Click on the listings and then carefully read the information in the post.
點選列表項目後閱讀廣告上的資訊。

 重要的資訊如：

contact information 聯絡資訊	**available date** 可入住日
deposit 押金	**minimum lease** 最短租賃期
included utilities 內含水電雜費	**property location** 房屋位置
features 房子特徵	**parking space** 停車位
amenities 設施	

Q 請聽音檔，並從中選出最符合圖片的敘述。

....

Script

A. The microwave is above the oven.

B. The stove is being used.

C. Stainless steel pots are hung on the wall.

D. The refrigerator is empty.

Answer A

Chapter 2

Making a Decision
作決定

在本章，你將會學習到如何對應自己所需，作出合適決定。

> **Situation: Select Places 挑選住處**
>
> 在上一章中，Carrie 蒐集了一大堆的資訊，可是面對這麼多的選擇，她到底該如何選出最適合自己需求的住所呢？

☆ 你能陪她一塊完成挑選嗎？

Work Schedule

⊘ List the Requirements 列出需求
⊘ Screen the Information 篩選資訊

TASK 1　List the Requirements

Prioritize Your Needs and Wants 將你的需求排序

五花八門的租屋資訊往往讓人不知從何下手，入眼的訊息量雖多，卻不見得都是自己所需要的。最有效率的方式，還是先列出自己的需求，再搭配預算，就不會愈看愈花啦。

Step 1

上一章我們學了很多租屋資訊，但你需要的是什麼？試著將你的需求填入下列空格。（答案因人而異）
In Chapter 1, we learned a lot of useful housing information. What are your needs? Try to fill in the blanks based on your requirements.

PRICING

Rent / Budget: $_____~_____ per month

Start Date: _____

Terms of the lease: _____ months / years

LOCATION

City: _____　　　　　State: _____

FEATURES

Number of Bedrooms: _____　Number of Full Bathrooms: _____

Floor in *Bldg (building): _____

Kitchen: Yes / No　　　　　Parking Space: Yes / No

AMENITIES

◆ _____　　　◆ _____
◆ _____　　　◆ _____
◆ _____　　　◆ _____

NEIGHBORHOOD

Nearby: ◆ _____　◆ _____　◆ _____

Step 2

列出你的各種需求後，接著從它們之中挑出最重要的五個排序吧！

So now that you have listed all your requirements, continue to prioritize your top five among them!

Step 3

回到 Carrie 的狀況，請幫她一起找出她的需求。

Back to Carrie's case, please help her find out her needs.

✐ **Exercise 1** 🎧 **Track 03**

請聽 Carrie 和 Paul 的對話，並於空格中填入適當的詞語。

- advice
- priorities
- set
- list
- rents
- features
- must-haves
- amenities
- suitable

Paul: What, Carrie, you're still here? How long have you been searching on the web, one or two hours?

Carrie: Actually, it's been three hours.

Paul: Unbelievable! Guess you must get what you need.

Carrie: To be honest, no. I got lost in the information. There are too many (1)_____ choices. How could I possibly go through all of them?

Paul: Didn't you (2)_____ your (3)_____?

Carrie: What do you mean? What priorities?

Paul: Before you start searching, it's important to sit down and (4)_____ everything you want for the house, including (5)_____, (6)_____, (7)_____, etc. Then choose your top five (8)_____. So you won't be stuck in the mess.

Carrie: Good (9)_____. Paul, I should have asked you earlier.

Paul: You really should. See how much time you wasted! Oh, use your priority list to help you stay on track while hunting.

Carrie: Alright, time for the list.

Paul: Need help?

🔑 Key Expressions

> 🔑 **To be honest = to tell the truth / to be frank** 坦白說
>
> 🔑 **got lost** 在此表示「迷失了」
>
> 🔑 **What do you mean?** 你的意思是？
>
> 🔑 **should have asked** 早該問 ★ should have + P.P. 表示應做而未做

🔑 Key Words

Word	Meaning
unbelievable (*a.*)	not to be believed 令人難以置信的
go through (*v. phr.*)	to examine carefully 檢視；討論
include (*v.*)	to have something as part of a group 包括
Idiom	**Meaning**
be stuck in the mess	caught or held in a position so that you cannot move from the mess 陷入一團混亂
stay on track	to stay on the path that one is on 維持（工作）進度

Answer

(1) suitable   (2) set   (3) priorities   (4) list   (5) features

(6) amenities   (7) rents   (8) must-haves   (9) advice

 Exercise 2 🎧 **Track 04**

請聽下列接續上述討論的對話，然後填入 Carrie 的需求。（有些答案會重複使用）

■ washing machine   ■ lower rent   ■ walking distance   ■ 950   ■ 30
■ convenient location   ■ Internet   ■ air-conditioning   ■ on-site laundry   ■ 2

Carrie: Alright, time for the list.

Paul: Need help?

Carrie: That'll be great!

Paul: OK, let's go through it one by one. First, think about the five must-haves.

Carrie: Uh ... I'll say (1) _____ , (2) _____ , (3) _____ ,
(4) _____ and (5) _____ .

Paul: Good. So now prioritize them.

Carrie: Of course number one is (6)_____. You know how expensive my <u>tuition</u> is. I can't afford an apartment more than $(7)_____ a month.

Paul: <u>Makes sense.</u>

Carrie: The second is ... (8)_____. It's too hard to live without the Net nowadays.

Paul: Very true. I can't imagine life without Google. And what's next?

Carrie: (9)_____. I don't want to walk a long way to do the laundry. <u>Especially</u> if I have to wait for an hour to bring it back.

Paul: Sounds like you prefer a washing machine at home. What about (10)_____?

Carrie: It's <u>acceptable</u>, but not my first choice.

Paul: Here comes the number four.

Carrie: I choose (11)_____. It should be close to my school. As I'm not going to buy a car there, the (12)_____ to the school should be no more than (13)_____ minutes.

Paul: Guess that's about (14)_____ miles, I think. So the last one is (15)_____?

Carrie: Yup, people say it's hot during the summer in LA, maybe hotter than Taiwan.

🔑 Key Words

Word	Meaning
tuition (*n.*)	money paid to a school for studying 學費
especially (*adv.*)	for a particular purpose 尤其；格外
acceptable (*a.*)	worthy of being accepted 可以接受的
Idiom	**Meaning**
make sense	to be reasonable 可理解的；很合理

Answer

(1) lower rent   (2) convenient location   (3) air-conditioning   (4) washing machine

(5) Internet   (6) lower rent   (7) 950   (8) Internet

(9) Washing machine   (10) on-site laundry   (11) convenient location (12) walking distance

(13) 30   (14) 2   (15) air-conditioning

TASK 2 Screen the Information

Comparison Chart 對照表

Step 1

Carrie 總算釐清了自己的需求，終於可以快速篩選目標啦！爲了能更有效率地運用找到資訊，建議作個表格來幫助比較喔。

Item	Price	Internet	Washing machine	Air-conditioning
Apt 1				
Apt 2				
Apt 3				

✏ Exercise 1

下面有三則廣告，試著使用上列表格填入以下各項資訊吧！（答案在第48頁）

Apt 1 STUDIO $825 FREE Wi-Fi + PARKING

Please call: Ronald 323-271-5676

Location: Long Beach, CA, 90802, 227 Olive Ave

Rent: $825

Deposit: $300

Available: February 23, 2014

Bedrooms: Studio
Bathrooms: 1 Bath
Furnished: No
Lease Type: Month-to-month lease
Structure Type: Apartments
Square Footage: 365
Parking: 1-car parking included

Amenities:
• Carpet and tile floors
• laundry on site
• refrigerator
• stove
• dishwasher
• patio
• controlled access building
• air conditioner

LARGE STUDIO with Private Patio - Water, Gas, Trash, are INCLUDED! Only $825! Water, Gas, and Trash are PAID!!! Cats Welcome - No Additional Deposit! Come by for a tour! Call and ask for Terry or email ty@argentx.net. We are open Mon - Sat 9am to 6pm Remodeled apartments include the following: • New carpet • New appliances • Two large laundry facilities (14 washers and dryers) • Professional on-site management • Controlled access / gated property • Elevators • Courtesy patrol • Free Wi-Fi.

Apt 2 GARDEN STUDIO IN COURTYARD

Please call: (562) 810-3403

Location: Long Beach, California. 90813, 1749 Cedar Ave

Rent: $900.00

Deposit: $900.00

Available: Available Now!

Bedrooms: Studio

Bathrooms: 1 Bath

Furnished: No

Lease Type: One year minimum lease

Pets: No pets

Structure Type: Apartments

Unit Details: Lower unit in 30-unit building

Parking: Parking available

Amenities:
• New Hardwood Floors
• laundry on site
• refrigerator
• stove
• controlled access building
• air conditioner
• high-speed Internet

New hardwood floor, new marble floor tiles in kitchen and bathroom. Re-glazed tub. Walk-in closet. Very quiet complex. Open floor plan. a/c, stove, and refrigerator. Across the street from Starbucks, Pavilions supermarket, restaurants, shops, and banks. Major bus stop close by. Clean. Gated entry to complex. Cable ready. Room for gardening. 3 washers and 3 dryers in laundry room. Please call for appointment.

Apt 3 1 BD / 1.0 BA UNIT IN HISTORICAL WILLMORE DISTRICT

Please Call: Office (562) 439-2147

Location: Long Beach, CA, 90804, 1119 Saint Louis Ave

Rent: $950.00

Deposit: $900

Available: Available Now!

Bedrooms: 1 Bedroom

Bathrooms: 1 Bath

Furnished: No

Lease Type: One year minimum lease

Pets: Cat ok

Structure Type: Apartments

Parking: 1-car Garage parking

Square Footage: 900

Amenities:
• Carpet floors
• stove
• yard
• washer + dryer

Fantastic building located in the Historical Willmore District. This charming apartment features an open living room/dining area, functional kitchen with stove and cabinets, and a good-sized bedroom. Also included are blinds, laundry, 1-car garage, and shared rear yard. Close to Pine Square, public transportation, and minutes to the beach! Located near 10th St and Pacific Ave.

Step 2

除了根據廣告上的訊息之外，Google Maps 也是非常好用的工具，可以幫助從未到過當地的你，更了解租屋地的區域位置、實際畫面，以及最重要的通勤距離。

Besides the information in the listing, Google Maps is another useful tool. Just enter the address of the house, and you can easily view its location, see a photo of the building, and calculate the commuting distance.

Apt 1: Long Beach, CA 90802, 227 Olive Ave

1. Location:

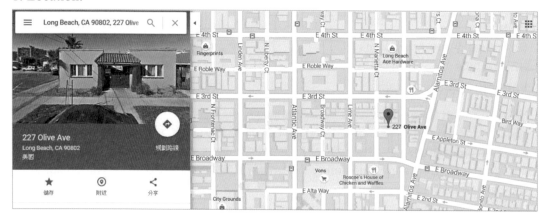

地圖資料 © 2016 Google

2. Google Street View

圖像拍攝日期 2 月 2015 © 2016 Google

3. Distance to Carrie's school (Long Beach City College)

地圖資料 © 2016 Google

根據上圖，預估從 Apt 1 到校的距離為 1.6 英哩，要走 31 分鐘左右。

✎ Exercise 2

現在換你試著將 Apt 2 和 Apt 3 的地址填入搜索引擎，實際看看現場地理環境，並將缺少的距離補上吧！

Apt 2: Long Beach, California. 90813, 1749 Cedar Ave
Apt 3: Long Beach, CA, 90804, 1119 Saint Louis Ave

Item	Walking Distance to Long Beach City College
Apt 1	1.6 miles / 31 minutes
Apt 2	
Apt 3	

Answer Exercise 1

Item	Price 租金	Internet 網路	Washing machine 洗衣機	Air-conditioning 空調
Apt 1	$825	Free Wi-Fi	laundry on site	Yes
Apt 2	$900	High-speed Internet	laundry on site	Yes
Apt 3	$950	No	washer + dryer	No

Answer Exercise 2 此答案僅供參考

Item	Walking Distance to Long Beach City College 至 Long Beach City College 的步行距離
Apt 1	1.6 miles / 31 minutes
Apt 2	1.3 miles / 26 minutes
Apt 3	1.0 miles / 20 minutes

Vocabulary Exercise

Task 1 Crossword Puzzle 填字遊戲

請根據下列英文提示，將該單字填入空格中。Hint: 可參考前面的 Key Words 表。

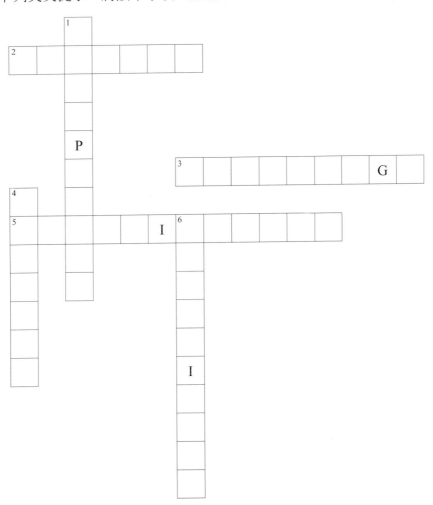

Down:

1. worthy of being accepted

4. money paid to a school for studying

6. for a particular purpose

Across:

2. to have something as part of a group

3. to examine carefully

5. not to be believed

Answer

1. acceptable   2. include   3. go through   4. tuition   5. unbelievable   6. especially

49

Task 2 Word Search 找字

請於下表中找出以下這些詞彙。Hint: 答案有可能是右到左或下到上排列。

- ACTUALLY
- ADVICE
- FEATURES
- SUITABLE
- MUST-HAVES
- PRIORITY

M	O	P	M	J	E	V	B	A	L	L	T	S	E	G
B	U	D	K	C	E	J	M	C	V	W	S	P	E	U
X	A	S	I	T	Z	L	X	T	J	S	E	H	Q	Q
Y	R	V	T	J	W	C	B	U	T	H	V	L	H	P
N	D	U	K	H	Z	G	W	A	P	U	R	D	Q	E
A	E	Q	K	F	A	N	Q	L	T	M	A	D	R	U
Q	F	D	L	O	W	V	P	L	Y	I	H	U	R	N
I	Z	C	H	B	Z	R	E	Y	Y	M	U	Q	E	V
U	C	O	O	G	I	W	Z	S	I	A	V	S	W	U
O	T	W	R	O	E	Y	C	Q	U	F	J	Z	R	W
S	S	E	R	U	T	A	E	F	H	W	E	K	R	N
Z	W	I	S	P	S	B	G	W	J	A	Y	C	X	V
O	T	N	A	L	V	Y	I	E	L	D	M	Z	H	M
Y	L	S	P	K	E	E	M	H	F	C	T	J	O	W
M	H	O	O	L	Q	H	L	X	E	V	M	Y	W	B

Answer

M	O	P	M	J	E	V	B	A	L	L	T	S	E	G
B	U	D	K	C	E	J	M	C	V	W	S	P	E	U
X	A	S	I	T	Z	L	X	T	J	S	E	H	Q	Q
Y	R	V	T	J	W	C	B	U	T	H	V	L	H	P
N	D	U	K	H	Z	G	W	A	P	U	R	D	Q	E
A	E	Q	K	F	A	N	Q	L	T	M	A	D	R	U
Q	F	D	L	O	W	V	P	L	Y	I	H	U	R	N
I	Z	C	H	B	Z	R	E	Y	Y	M	U	Q	E	V
U	C	O	O	G	I	W	Z	S	I	A	V	S	W	U
O	T	W	R	O	E	Y	C	Q	U	F	J	Z	R	W
S	S	E	R	U	T	A	E	F	H	W	E	K	R	N
Z	W	I	S	P	S	B	G	W	J	A	Y	C	X	V
O	T	N	A	L	V	Y	I	E	L	D	M	Z	H	M
Y	L	S	P	K	E	E	M	H	F	C	T	J	O	W
M	H	O	O	L	Q	H	L	X	E	V	M	Y	W	B

List your housing requirements before searching.
上網搜尋前,先列出租屋需求。

 常見大標如:

Pricing 租金、押金等   **Location** 位置距離   **Features** 房屋特徵

Amenities 房屋設施   **Neighborhood** 鄰近環境

可按照這幾項大標,依序細想自己的需要。

↓

Prioritize the requirements you listed.
將列出的需求,按其重要性排列。

↓

Screen the information and fill in a comparison chart.
進行篩選,將資訊填入表格內比較。

↓

Use Google Maps to perform a more detailed search on the location and environment. 運用 Google Maps 對當地環境位置進行更詳細的探索。

※ 這對僅能在網路搜尋、對該地完全陌生的你,可是檢視租屋地非常有用的一步呢!

TOEIC Test

🎧 Track 05

Q 請聽音檔播放的問題，並以四到五個句子回答。

Script

What household amenities are necessary for you?

Answer 參考答案

As LA is super hot in the summer, air-conditioning plays a key role in my house. Also, having a washer and dryer saves me a lot of time compared with hand-washing. They, therefore, are the must-haves. But if I'm only allowed to keep one amenity, I'll say it's high-speed Internet. From schoolwork to daily life, it's used everywhere. No Internet, no life.

Chapter 3

Making an Appointment
約定看屋

在本章，你將會學習到如何用 email 和電話聯繫預約看屋。

Situation: Contact the Landlord / Agent
聯繫房東或仲介

在網路上找尋到了合適的幾間公寓後，接著當然就是和廣告上面的聯絡人聯繫看屋啦！但對 Carrie 來說，一想到要和外國人聯繫，可是冷汗直冒呢！

☆ 你能陪她一塊完成這些聯繫動作嗎？

Work Schedule

⊘ Contact via Email Email 聯繫

⊘ Contact via Phone 電話聯繫

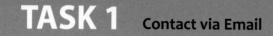

TASK 1　Contact via Email

The Most Economic Way 最經濟的聯絡方式

想找房子雖說透過網站搜尋相當方便，但可不能單單靠著網上的資訊就夠了，還是得要親自到現場一探究竟才行。不過看房子畢竟不是說去就去的，還得和聯繫人約好時間地點，才能順利參觀。雖然打電話是最快的方式，但若是人在國外，透過 email 先做好安排才是最省錢又省力的作法。

Step 1

寫 email 前，除了再把廣告瀏覽一遍，寫下想詢問的問題，還有什麼是你應該注意的呢？
Review the rental advertisement and then write down the questions you'd like to ask. Is there anything else you should pay attention on the ads?

Email 範例：

> Dear Mr. Murray,
> I saw you have an apartment in Los Angeles for rent on Craigslist.

重點：
1. 確認聯絡人姓名　　2. 寫下租屋資訊來源處　　3. 寫下租屋資訊

✎ Exercise 1

請看下面這則 Carrie 所挑選出的廣告之一，幫她想想有什麼問題需要提出呢？
（翻譯在第217頁）

$700 Huge apartments at an affordable price! Hurry in!

RENTAL INFO

Rental Rates: $700/month

Location: 3101 E Artesia Blvd Long Beach, CA 90805

Unit for Rent: Studio | Square feet: 360 ft | Lease Length: 12-Months

---

```
LIST OF AMENITIES
Community
    - Covered Parking      - On-site Management      - Assigned Parking
Unit Features
    - Some Utilities Paid    - Wall Unit Air Conditioning
    - Sliding Shower Doors  - Ceiling Fan(s)          - Carpet
ADDITIONAL INFO
Contact Leasing Office:
www.apts123.net/rent.aspx?p=5C7cyQSu6ck%3d


Artesia Apartments: (562) 506-1929
```

可能問題：

1. 押金多少：＿＿＿＿＿＿＿＿＿＿ is the deposit?

2. 公共設施（如水電瓦斯）哪些不需付費：＿＿＿＿＿＿＿＿＿ of utilities is paid?

3. 有洗衣房嗎：＿＿＿＿＿＿＿＿ any on-site laundry?

4. 屋內還有附哪些傢俱：＿＿＿＿＿＿ other rental unit features ＿＿＿＿＿＿＿？

5. 其他：＿＿＿＿＿＿＿＿＿＿＿＿＿＿＿＿＿＿＿＿＿＿＿＿＿＿＿＿＿

Answer

1. **How much** is the deposit?

2. **What part** of the utilities is paid?

3. **Is there** any on-site laundry?

4. **What** other rental unit features **are there**?

5. Does the toilet flush properly? Are the hot and cold water working well?

   馬桶沖水和冷熱水系統運作良好嗎？

   Do the air conditioner and fans look in good working condition? 冷氣機和風扇狀態良好嗎？

Step 2

接著，確認自己能夠前往看屋的時間，最好可以多預留幾個時段。

Check your schedule to see when you are available to make a visit. It's better to have more than one possible time.

以下是 Carrie 所能空出來的看屋時段，在 email 中該如何表明呢？

Available Time	Mon (8/20)	Tue (8/21)	Wed (8/22)	Thu (8/23)	Fri (8/24)
Morning		10-12 pm		10-11 am	
Afternoon			1-3 pm	3-5 pm	
Evening					

2-1. 請先仿照 1 將下列時間以英文表示。

1. Tue (10-12 pm): <u>Tuesday 10-12 pm / Tuesday from 10 am to 12 pm</u>（完整寫法）

2. Wed (1-3 pm): _____

3. Thu (10-11 am): _____

4. Thu (3-5 pm): _____

Answer

2. Wednesday 1-3 pm / Wednesday from 1 pm to 3 pm

3. Thursday 10-11 am / Thursday from 10 am to 11 am

4. Thursday 3-5 pm / Thursday from 3 pm to 5 pm

2-2. 因為提供時段較多，為便於瀏覽，建議可用如上述般條列式的方式表明，在最前面則加上一句：

「以下這些時段您何時有空協助看屋？」

<u>Which of the following times are you available to assist an on-site visit?</u>

1. Tuesday 10-12 pm

2. Wednesday 1-3 pm

3. Thursday 10-11 am

4. Thursday 3-5 pm

Step 3

準備工作都已完成，差不多可以開始寫信了。信的開頭，不能免俗地要來段簡短的自我介紹。

Now the preparation work is done. We are ready to write the email. But don't forget, at the beginning of the letter, we still need a brief self-introduction.

✎ Exercise 3

Carrie 想好了要問的問題，也確認好了能看屋的時間。Carrie 終於可以開始動手寫信，不過信開頭的自我介紹該怎麼寫呢？

自我介紹範例：

> I am a <u>newly arrived international</u> student in search of a temporary place to <u>live while I finish my graduate studies</u>. I will be living in the <u>Long Beach</u> area for 2-3 years.
> 我是新來的國際學生，正在 Long Beach 尋找未來兩三年的短期住處以完成研究所學業。

請仿照 Carrie 的句子，寫出你自己的答案：

I am a _____（身分）in search of a temporary place
to _____（目的）. I will be living in the
_____（地區）area for 2-3 years.

✎ Exercise 4

終於到了信末，Carrie 得附上自己的聯絡資訊，以便屋主聯繫。你的資訊呢？

Please contact me at _____（電話號碼）or via email:
_____（信箱地址）.

 **Key Expressions**

詢問對方空閒時間的方式還有以下幾種常見句型：（空格中填入合適的時間）

Asking to Meet			
Are you available	on / at		?
Are you free	on / at		?
Is			OK?
Is			good for you ?
Is			**convenient** for you?
Would			be OK?
Would			**suit** you?
Can we meet	on / at		?
Can you manage			?
How does			sound to you?

* **on** 用於星期、日期：on Friday / on May 3rd

  at 用於時間：at 2:30 / at 3 o'clock

  一起使用時：on Friday at 2:30

** 要小心的是 **next** 前面不要使用任何介系詞：next Monday

Key Words

Word	Meaning
properly (*adv.*)	suitably; fittingly 適當地
work well (*v. phr.*)	to perform a job well 運作良好
in good condition (*phr.*)	physically and functionally sound 狀態良好
newly arrived (*a.*)	recently arrived 新進的
international (*a.*)	across nations 國際的
temporary (*a.*)	lasting for a time only 短暫的
graduate studies (*n. phr.*)	relating to studies taken after a bachelor's degree 研究所課程
convenient (*a.*)	for someone to do something easily or without trouble 方便的
suit (*v.*)	to fit 適合

TASK 2 Contact via Phone

The Fastest Way 最快速的聯絡方式

若是寫信太麻煩，或是對方沒有附上 email 信箱，也可以直接打電話聯繫。接著來看看 Carrie 怎麼和對方預約吧！

Exercise 1 🎧 Track 06

請聽 Carrie 和房東預約看屋的對話，並將聽到的訊息填入空格中。

- Tuesday and Friday
- email address
- abcd123@gmail.com
- view the studio
- Tuesday, the 21ˢᵗ
- Tuesday morning
- Tuesday afternoon
- 10 o'clock

Carrie: Hey, my name is Carrie. I'd like to make an appointment with the <u>landlord</u> to
(1) _____ next week.

Landlord: Hi, this is Jay. I'm the landlord. Let me check my <u>schedule book</u> ... next week ...
Yes, I have (2) _____ available. Which day would you prefer?

Carrie: Um ... I'd like to meet on (3) _____.

Landlord: OK. Can you come in the afternoon?

Carrie: Oh ... I'm sorry. I can't make it (4) _____. Can you <u>manage</u>
(5) _____?

Landlord: Yes, morning is fine too.

Carrie: Great! So let's say (6) _____ in the morning?

Landlord: Sounds good. Can you bring me your <u>ID</u> when you come?

Carrie: Sure. Anything else?

Landlord: No, that's all I need. Do you know how to get here?

Carrie: No, I need the <u>directions</u>.

Landlord: Do you have an (7) _____? I can send you the information you need.

Carrie: Excellent. Do you have a pen and paper?

Landlord: Yes, please.

Carrie: It's (8) _____.

Landlord: OK, let me repeat that to make sure if I got it right. It's (9) _____.

Carrie: That's correct. I'll <u>look forward to</u> the email. Bye.

Landlord: Bye.

🔑 Key Expressions

📝 **I'd like to make an appointment to ....** 我想預約……。

   = **Is it possible to make an appointment to ...?**

   = **May I make an appointment to ...?**

📝 **I have ... available.** 我……有空。

   = **I'm available on/at ....**

📝 **Which day would you prefer?** 哪天比較好？（底線部分可自換時間）

   = **Which is better for you, <u>Monday</u> or <u>Friday</u>?**

   = **Would you prefer <u>Monday</u> or <u>Friday</u>?**

   = **What day would be best for you?**

📝 **I can't make it ....** 我……不行。

   = **I can't do ....**

📝 **Can you manage ...?** 你可以安排……嗎？

   = **Can you arrange ...? = Can you schedule ...?**

📝 **... is fine.** ……可以。

   = **... is OK. = ... sounds good. = I'm fine with ....**

📝 **Let's say ....** 那約……。

   = **How about ...? = What about ...?**

🔑 Key Words

Word	Meaning
landlord (*n.*)	the person who owns or rents buildings or lands 房東
schedule book (*n.*)	a book that writes a series of things to be done or of events to occur in a certain time or period 行事曆
manage (*v.*)	to work upon or try to alter for a purpose 安排
ID [identification] (*n.*)	a document to show your personal information 身分證件
direction (*n.*)	instructions that tell you how to go to a place 方向
look forward to (*v. phr.*)	to think of a future event with eagerness or pleasure 期待

Answer

(1) view the studio   (2) Tuesday and Friday   (3) Tuesday, the 21st   (4) Tuesday afternoon

(5) Tuesday morning   (6) 10 o'clock   (7) email address   (8) abcd123@gmail.com

(9) abcd123@gmail.com

✏ Exercise 2

電話中，房東請 Carrie 攜帶身分證件前往。不僅 Carrie 想挑好屋子，房東也想挑個好房客！除了個人基本資料外，一般還會攜帶個人履歷 (resume)，履歷上 Carrie 還需要寫些什麼呢？（[ ] 部分請依照你的需求改寫）

For the past [four] years I've rented a [small apartment] in [the north of Taiwan]. I always [treat a rental place as my own], and [take the care and maintenance of both the interior and the exterior very seriously].

Now that I am now moving to [Long Beach], I would like to look for a [studio] close to [my school]. [Your studio] is my primary choice because of its [good layout] and [its proximity to the bus stop and Long Beach City University]. Attached are my [financial statement and credit report] which show [my ability to pay the rent on time].

過去四年，我於台灣北部租賃一間小公寓。我總把租屋處當成自己家一樣，認真維護內外環境。我現在搬到 Long Beach，想找一間靠近學校的 studio。因為格局完善，且離公車站及 Long Beach 大學都近，您出租的 studio 是我的第一選擇。隨信附上我的財力證明和信用報告。

請仿照 Carrie 的句子，寫出你自己的答案：

For the past _____（時間）I've rented a _____（房型）in _____（租屋地）. I always _____ （自己租屋時的優點 1）, and _____ （自己租屋時的優點 2）very seriously.

Now that I am now moving to _____（新地點), I would like to look for a _____（房型）close to _____ （離哪近）. Your _____（出租的房屋）is my primary choice because of its _____ （優點 1）and _____ （優點 2）. Attached are _____（有益租屋的文件） which show _____（文件功能）.

＊描述你過去的租屋經驗如何，以及為何選擇對方的原因，可以讓房東更了解你！

🔑 Key Words

Word	Meaning
resume (*n.*)	a short document describing your personal background 履歷
treat (sth) as ...	to regard or deal with something in a certain way 當作；視為
take (sth) seriously	to carry out in an earnest manner 認真對待某事
maintenance (*n.*)	keeping in good condition 維持；保養
interior (*n.*)	located inside a building 內部
exterior (*n.*)	located outside a building 外部
now that (*conj.*)	since 既然
primary (*a.*)	being or standing first in a list 首要的
layout (*n.*)	the design or arrangement of a house 格局
proximity (*n.*)	the state of being near, close 鄰近
financial statement (*n.*)	a document showing credits and debits 財力證明
credit report (*n.*)	a detailed report of an individual's credit history prepared by a credit bureau 信用報告

Task 1 Crossword Puzzle 填字遊戲

請根據下列英文提示，將該單字填入空格中。Hint: 可參考前面的 Key Words 表。

Across:

1. instructions that tell you how to go to a place

4. being or standing first in a list

7. lasting for a time only

9. located inside a building

12. to fit

14. keeping in good condition

Down:

2. located outside a building

3. to work upon or try to alter for a purpose

5. the design or arrangement of a house

6. the person who owns or rents buildings or lands

8. the state of being near, close

10. a short document describing your personal background

11. suitably; fittingly

13. for someone to do something easily or without trouble

....

Task 2 Scrambled Words 字母重組

請將左方亂序的字母重組成有意義的單字，最後再將各個數字裡的字母填入最後一欄。

1 PORRYEPL

2 CEVNEITONN

3 TISU

4 RARPYTEMO

5 DOLLDARN

6 GEAMAN

7 DINRIETOC

8 MEETIACANNN

☐☐☐☐☐☐☐☐☐☐☐
    4

9 ROTNIERI

☐☐☐☐☐☐☐☐

10 EIXOTERR

☐☐☐☐☐☐☐☐

11 LUTYAO

☐☐☐☐☐☐

12 TIXROMPYI

☐☐☐☐☐☐☐☐☐
        1

☐☐☐☐☐☐
1 2 3 4 5 6

Ch
3

Answer

1 properly   2 convenient   3 suit   4 temporary   5 landlord   6 manage

7 direction   8 maintenance   9 interior   10 exterior   11 layout   12 proximity

最後一欄組合起來的單字是 manage

67

 Review the rental advertisement and write down the questions you want to ask. 先瀏覽一遍廣告,寫下想詢問的問題。

↓

Check your schedule to see when you are available to visit the house. 確認一下自己能前往看屋的時間。 ★別忘了多預留幾個時段做選擇。

↓   ↓

Write an email to make an appointment.
開始寫信預約看屋。

 信的開頭還是要來段簡短自我介紹喔! Email 內文順序:
① 自我介紹並表達目的
② 想詢問的問題
③ 提供自己方便看屋的時段
④ 聯繫電話或信箱

Make a phone call to schedule an appointment. 直接打電話預約看屋。

 常用表達句型:
① I'd like to make an appointment to ....
我想預約⋯⋯。
② I have ... available. 我⋯⋯有空。
③ Which day would you prefer?
哪天比較好?
④ I can't make it .... 我⋯⋯不行。
⑤ Can you manage ...? 你可以安排⋯⋯嗎?
⑥ ... is fine. ⋯⋯可以。
⑦ Let's say .... 那約⋯⋯。

↓

Bring your ID and resume when you visit the house. 攜帶身分證件和履歷前往。

 可描述你過去的租屋經驗如何,包含:
① 證明自己是個好房客的例子
② 為何選擇對方的原因
③ 附帶文件

Q 請根據下圖寫出一個句子，句中須使用所給予的單字。單字可改變時態、詞性和順序。

layout / design

Answer 參考答案

The layout of the studio is well designed.

Chapter 4

Transportation
交通

在本章，你將會學習到如何搭乘交通工具和問路。

Situation: Visit the Apartment 前往看屋

和屋主聯繫好時間後，接著當然就是要前往看屋，但 Carrie 是第一次到該地，人生地不熟的，雖有地址和地圖，但該搭乘什麼交通工具，以及怎麼搭乘，這可考倒 Carrie 了。

☆ 你能陪她一塊完成這些交通行程嗎？

Work Schedule

⊘ Take Public Transportation 搭乘大眾運輸工具

⊘ Ask for Directions 問路

TASK 1　Take Public Transportation

Metro + Bus 捷運和公車

雖說找地方最方便就是搭計程車，但往往所費不貲。而現在城鎮內的大眾交通工具資訊多已網路化，事前上網查找就能妥善安排路線，順手把資訊存在手機裡或列印出來，到時跟著走就對啦！

Step 1

在 LA 搭乘 Metro（大眾運輸系統）其實跟在台北一樣簡易，只要進入 LA Metro 的網站就可以查詢到所有你需要的乘車資訊。

Using the LA Metro is as easy as taking public transportation in Taipei. Just open the LA Metro website, and you can get all the transit information you need.

\<Website\> http://www.metro.net/

註 雖然網站內有中文，但規劃路線還是得靠英文唷。

Step 2

有了出發地和目的地，來幫幫 Carrie 規劃前進路線吧！

With the starting point and the destination, let's plan the trip for Carrie!

註 出發地和目的地的填法有：地址、交叉路口、地標

Starting point: LAX CITY BUS CENTER

Destination: 227 Olive Ave, Long Beach, CA 90802 (Apt 1 address on p. 44)

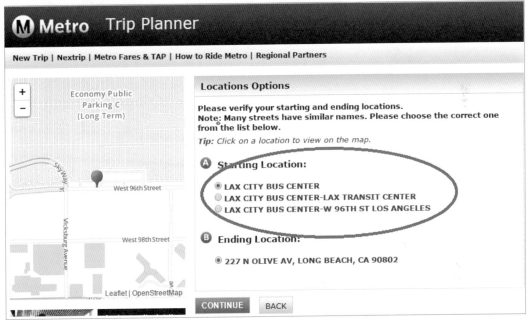

Step 3

結果出現了三個出發地,該選哪個好呢?試著點擊這三個地點,瞧瞧左邊地圖的
變化吧!

Which one should you choose among these three starting locations? Click them and see what
happens to the map on the left.

Answer

基本上三個地點距離差不多,選哪個都可以喔!

Step 4

確定出發地和目的地後，接著按下 continue（繼續）鍵。結果又是選擇題，且路程時間只給了大概範圍，看來想確認哪條路線花費時間最少，可得一個一個點進去看了！

Click the "continue" button for further information. Choices again! Since the estimated trip time is given in a range, we can only find out the shortest route by clicking on each "Details" to see the information.

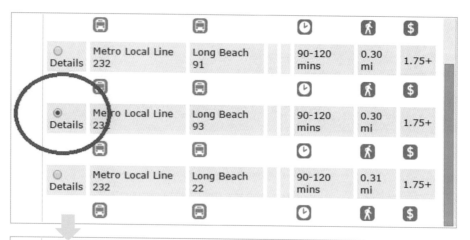

Ride **Metro Local Line 232** [DOWNTOWN LONG BEACH] heading west

From: LAX CITY BUS CTR/BUS BAY 8 Lv: **09:00AM**

To: LONG BEACH BLVD/3RD ST SW corner Ar: **10:47AM**

Pay $1.75 + $0.50 for Transfer., Monthly Pass: $100.00, EZ Pass accepted

Ride **Long Beach 93** [ALONDRA & WOODRUFF] heading north

From: LONG BEACH BLVD/3RD ST SE corner Lv: **11:07AM**

To: 6TH ST/OLIVE AV SE corner Ar: **11:12AM**

Use Transfer or Media , Monthly Pass: $65.00, EZ Pass accepted

---

Ending at 227 N OLIVE AV
Find Nearby... Pass/TAP Outlets | Park & Ride Lots

Additional Information

Total fare = $2.25

Trip time is about **2** hours and **12** minutes.

Trip distance is about **24.55** miles.

*All times are approximate. Traffic and weather can cause delays.
Please allow extra time for boarding and alighting.

✐ Exercise 1

試試點擊其他行程的 "Details"，進去找看看哪個路程時間最短？

....

Answer

第一個，花費 1 小時 52 分鐘。

Step 5

終於，詳細路線和價錢都出來了。有沒有發現，LA 的公車都是停在交叉路口呢！
Finally, here are the directions and fare. Have you noticed that all the buses stop at an intersection?

註 兩條街的交叉路口，表示上多以斜線來區隔，例如：6TH ST/OLIVE AV 代表 6TH 街和 OLIVE 大道交叉路口。若是要在 Google Maps 上查詢的話，斜線請改成 and(&) 喔！

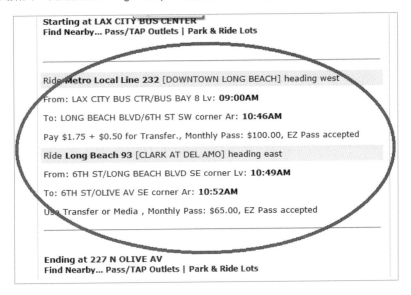

Starting at LAX CITY BUS CENTER
Find Nearby... Pass/TAP Outlets | Park & Ride Lots

_____

Ride **Metro Local Line 232** [DOWNTOWN LONG BEACH] heading west

From: LAX CITY BUS CTR/BUS BAY 8 Lv: **09:00AM**

To: LONG BEACH BLVD/6TH ST SW corner Ar: **10:46AM**

Pay $1.75 + $0.50 for Transfer., Monthly Pass: $100.00, EZ Pass accepted

Ride **Long Beach 93** [CLARK AT DEL AMO] heading east

From: 6TH ST/LONG BEACH BLVD SE corner Lv: **10:49AM**

To: 6TH ST/OLIVE AV SE corner Ar: **10:52AM**

Use Transfer or Media , Monthly Pass: $65.00, EZ Pass accepted

_____

Ending at 227 N OLIVE AV
Find Nearby... Pass/TAP Outlets | Park & Ride Lots

✐ Exercise 2

請根據 Step 5 的資訊，回答以下問題。

▉ How many times does Carrie need to transfer?

▉ How much does Carrie need to pay for the whole trip?

▉ At which station does Carrie need to transfer?

....

Answer

☐ 1 time   ☐ $2.25   ☐ LONG BEACH BLVD/6TH ST

請看下面有關車費的描述後，回答問題。（翻譯在第218頁）

Metro's base fare is $1.50. You can pay cash each time you board a Metro bus (bus operators don't carry change, so you'll need exact fare) or buy and add value to a reusable TAP card from TAP vending machines at Metro Rail or Metro Orange Line stations.

Reduced cash fares are available for seniors and disabled riders with valid proof of status.

> TIP: Two children under age 5 may travel free with each fare paying adult on bus or rail.

If you're going to be a frequent rider, a Monthly or Weekly Pass may be your best value. There are several types of Reduced Fare Passes for students, seniors and disabled riders as well; a Day Pass is also available. All are sold on stored value cards called TAP cards at hundreds of locations throughout the county.

> TIP: If you're getting on a Metro bus with a prepaid pass or stored value on a TAP card, simply tap it on the farebox's TAP target as you board. On Metro Rail lines and the Metro Orange Line, you need to tap your card on the turnstile or station validator as you enter the station.

<Website> http://www.metro.net/riding/getting-started/

1 How much is the base fare?

2 Can you get change back from a bus driver?

3 What is a TAP card?

4 Where can you buy a TAP card?

5 Whose cash fares can be reduced?

6 If you are a frequent rider, what are some other fare plans good for you?

7 If you bring a 3-year-old child on a Metro bus, does the child need to pay?

8 How do you use a TAP card on a Metro bus?

Key Words

Word	Meaning
fare (*n.*)	a transportation charge 票價;車費
board (*v.*)	to get into or onto (an airplane, a bus, a train, etc.) 上車、船、機等
operator (*n.*)	a person who uses and controls something 司機;操作者
change (*n.*)	money returned when a payment is more than the amount due 找零;零錢
exact (*a.*)	fully and completely correct or accurate 準確的;精確的
value (*n.*)	the price or cost of something 價值;價格
reusable (*a.*)	able to be used again 可重複使用的
vending machine (*n.*)	a machine that you put money into in order to buy food, drinks, etc. 販賣機
reduce (*v.*)	to make (sth) smaller in size, amount, number, etc. 減少;降低
senior (*a.*)	a person who is older than others 年長的
disabled (*a.*)	unable to perform one or more natural activities (such as walking or seeing) because of illness, injury, etc. 行動不便的
valid (*a.*)	acceptable according to the law 合法的;有效的
proof (*n.*)	something which shows that something else is true or correct 證據
status (*n.*)	the condition of a person or thing in the eyes of the law 身分;地位
frequent (*a.*)	to visit or go to (a place) often 經常的
store (*v.*)	to reserve or put away for future use 貯存
throughout (*adv.*)	in or to every part, everywhere 遍及
prepaid (*a.*)	to pay for (sth) before you receive or use it 預付的
tap (*v.*)	to strike gently with a light blow 輕拍;輕敲
target (*n.*)	a mark to shoot at 目標;靶子

Ch
4

Answer

1 Metro's base fare is $1.50.

2 No, bus operators don't carry change, so you'll need exact fare.

3 TAP cards are stored value cards.

4 Hundreds of locations throughout the county

5 Seniors and disabled riders

6 A Monthly or Weekly Pass

7 No, two children under age 5 may travel free with each fare paying adult on bus or rail.

8 Simply tap a TAP card on the farebox's TAP target as you board.

有了乘車資訊，Carrie 放心多了，不過從飯店 (Hilton Los Angeles Airport) 出發時到底該怎麼走到公車站。Carrie 看著地圖站在路上不知所措，看來得開口請路人幫幫忙了。

✎ Exercise 1　🎧 Track 07

請聽 Carrie 和路人的對話，並於空格中填入適當的詞語。

- LAX City Bus Center　- W 96th St　- Airport Dr　- 300　- 4 to 5
- W Century Blvd　- right　- right　- left　- Metro Local Line 232

Carrie: Excuse me. I'm looking for (1)＿＿＿＿＿, the bus stop for (2)＿＿＿＿＿. Do you know where it is?

Passerby: Oh, it's not far from here. Go down (3)＿＿＿＿＿ and turn right on Airport Dr.

Carrie: Turn (4)＿＿＿＿＿ on (5)＿＿＿＿＿. OK.

Passerby: Keep going straight down Airport Dr for two blocks to (6)＿＿＿＿＿.

Carrie: How long will that be?

Passerby: About (7)＿＿＿＿＿ yards, like (8)＿＿＿＿＿ minutes?

Carrie: I see, and then?

Passerby: Then take a (9)＿＿＿＿＿ on W 96th St. You'll see the bus stop is on your (10)＿＿＿＿＿-hand side.

Carrie: Great! It sounds very easy.

Passerby: It is easy. Don't worry. You won't miss it.

Carrie: Thank you.

Passerby: No problem.

....

Answer

(1) LAX City Bus Center　(2) Metro Local Line 232　(3) W Century Blvd　(4) right　(5) Airport Dr
(6) W 96th St　　　　　　(7) 300　　　　　　　　　(8) 4 to 5　　　　　　(9) left　(10) right

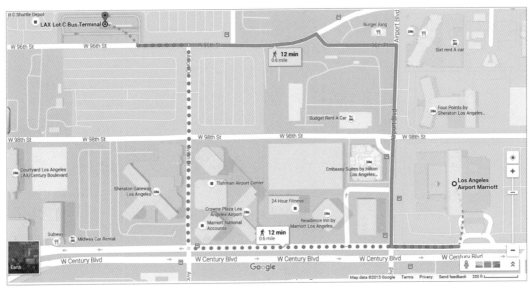

地圖資料 © 2016 Google

✎ Exercise 2   🎧 Track 08

請聽另一段 Carrie 和路人的對話，並於空格中填入適當的詞語。

■ E Broadway   ■ Olive Ave   ■ right   ■ 227 Olive Ave   ■ 300   ■ a block

Carrie: Excuse me, are you from here?

Passerby: Yes.

Carrie: Great. I'm looking for this address: (1)_____. Could you tell me how to
           get there?

Passerby: 227 Olive Ave? Oh, yeah, I know where that is. Walk along (2)_____
           and turn (3)_____ on (4)_____.

Carrie: OK, turn right. What's next?

Passerby: Then keep walking on Olive Ave. It's about (5)_____ away.

Carrie: Wow, that sounds pretty close.

Passerby: Actually, it is. It's only about (6)_____ yards I think.

Carrie: Guess I won't get lost. Thanks!

Passerby: Don't mention it.

....

Answer

(1) 227 Olive Ave   (2) E Broadway   (3) right   (4) Olive Ave   (5) a block   (6) 300

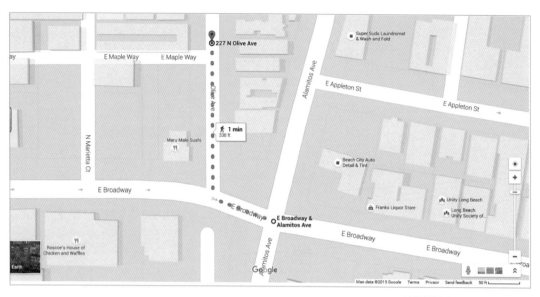

地圖資料 © 2016 Google

向人問路的方式有以下幾種常見句型：（空格中填入要詢問的地點）

Asking for Directions		
Excuse me,	would/could you tell me	how to get to _____ ?
	do you know	where _____ is?
	I'm looking for _____ .	
	how do I get to _____ ?	
	what is the best/easiest/quickest way to get to _____ ?	
	where is _____ ?	
	can you give me directions to _____ ?	
	is there _____ around here? （詢問附近是否有你需要的場所）	
Asking for Distance		
Excuse me,	is _____ far from here?	
	how long will it take to get to _____ ?	

✐ **Exercise 3-1**

挑選幾個上面的句型，試試看問車站怎麼去吧。

1 _____

2 _____

3 _____

✐ **Exercise 3-2**

接著問問看車站距離有多遠呢？

1 _____

2 _____

🔑 **Key Expressions**

而向人報路的表達方式有以下數種：（空格中根據需要填入路名 [street name]、地標 [landmark] 或時間 [time] 與距離 [mile] 等。）

Giving Directions					
直行	Go straight	on	(street name)	for	(time) (miles) (blocks)
	Go	down	(street name)		
繼續直行	Continue/Stay	on	(street name)		
	Keep going	on	(street name)		
左 / 右轉	Turn left/right	on	(street name)		
		at	(landmark)		
左 / 右轉	Take a left/right	on	(street name)		
		at	(landmark)		
		after you pass	(landmark)		
		when you see / get to	(landmark)/ (street name)		

再一次左 / 右轉	Take another right/left	on	(street name)	
過幾個路口	Go _____ blocks	to	(street name)	
越過	Cross		(street name)	
經過	Go past		(landmark)	

表示位置的方式則如下，可一次運用多個。

		over there		
（目的地）	is	just around the corner		
		next to	(landmark)	
		across from	(landmark)	
		in front of	(landmark)	
		opposite	(landmark)	
		beside	(landmark)	
		between	(landmark A)	and	(landmark B)
		on the corner of	(street A)	and	(street B)
		on the left/right		

Answer Exercise 3-1 （任選三）

Excuse me, would/could you tell me how to get to the train station?

Excuse me, would/could you tell me where the train station is?

Excuse me, do you know how to get to the train station?

Excuse me, do you know where the train station is?

Excuse me, I'm looking for the train station.

Excuse me, how do I get to the train station?

Excuse me, what is the best/easiest/quickest way to get to the train station?

Excuse me, where is the train station?

Excuse me, can you give me directions to the train station?

Answer Exercise 3-2

Excuse me, is the train station far from here?

Excuse me, how long will it take to get to the train station?

✎ Exercise 4

試試看運用上面的表達方式寫出下列指引：

沿著忠孝東路 (Zhongxiao E. Rd) 直走三分鐘，之後右轉仁愛路 (Ren'ai Rd)。當你看到 7-11 時再一次右轉，然後經過第一銀行，你就會看到餐廳在右手邊，Strabucks 的隔壁。

_____

_____

_____

_____

_____

_____

Answer

Go straight on Zhongxiao E. Rd for 3 minutes, and turn right on Ren'ai Rd. Take another right when you see the 7-11. Then go past the First Bank. You'll see the restaurant on the right, next to the Starbucks.

Task 1 Crossword Puzzle 填字遊戲

請根據下列英文提示，將該單字填入空格中。Hint: 可參考前面的 Key Words 表。

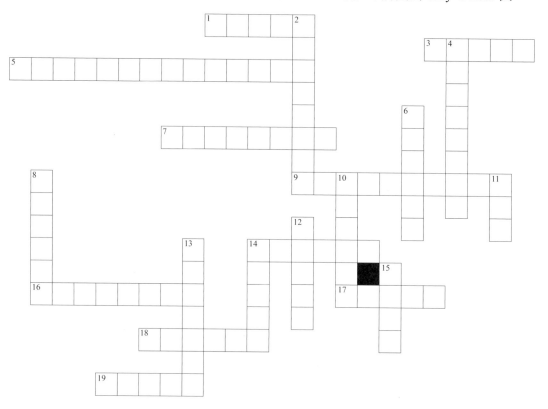

Across:

1. something which shows that something else is true or correct

3. to get into or onto (an airplane, a bus, a train, etc.)

5. a machine that you put money into in order to buy food, drinks, etc.

7. unable to perform one or more natural activities (such as walking or seeing) because of illness, injury, etc.

9. in or to every part, everywhere

14. the condition of a person or thing in the eyes of the law

16. able to be used again

17. fully and completely correct or accurate

18. money returned when a payment is more than the amount due

19. acceptable according to the law

Down:

2. to visit or go to (a place) often

4. a person who uses and controls something

6. a mark to shoot at

8. a person who is older than others

10. to make (sth) smaller in size, amount, number, etc.

11. to strike gently with a light blow

12. the price or cost of something

13. to pay for (sth) before you receive or use it

14. to reserve or put away for future use

15. transportation charge

....

Answer

1. proof	2. frequent	3. board	4. operator	5. vending machine
6. target	7. disabled	8. senior	9. throughout	10. reduce
11. tap	12. value	13. prepaid	14. status (ACROSS)	14. store (DOWN)
15. fare	16. reusable	17. exact	18. change	19. valid

Task 2 Matching 配對

請於右列的英文字中，找出和左方的中文字義相對應者。

1 販賣機 _____	A disabled
2 遍及 _____	B board
3 行動不便的 _____	C prepaid
4 經常的 _____	D reusable
5 司機 _____	E tap
6 可重複使用的 _____	F operator
7 預付的 _____	G valid
8 零錢 _____	H frequent
9 減少 _____	I status
10 年長的 _____	J fare
11 身分 _____	K proof
12 目標 _____	L reduce
13 上車 _____	M value
14 精確的 _____	N change
15 證據 _____	O senior
16 貯存 _____	P target
17 有效的 _____	Q store
18 價值 _____	R exact
19 車費 _____	S vending machine
20 輕敲 _____	T throughout

Answer

1 販賣機 S	2 遍及 T	3 行動不便的 A	4 經常的 H	5 司機 F
6 可重複使用的 D	7 預付的 C	8 零錢 N	9 減少 L	10 年長的 O
11 身分 I	12 目標 P	13 上車 B	14 精確的 R	15 證據 K
16 貯存 Q	17 有效的 G	18 價值 M	19 車費 J	20 輕敲 E

With the starting point and destination in hand, open the LA Metro website to plan the trip.
知道出發地和目的地後，進入 LA Metro 的網站規畫你的行程吧。

※ 若有需要可利用 Google Maps 查詢最短程的路線。

Calculate the distance and price. 計算路程和金額以做安排。

Follow the instructions to your destination. If you get lost, be brave and ask for directions!
跟著指示前往你的目的地。找不到路的時候，勇敢開口問路吧！

🖉 常用問路句型：

① **Excuse me, would/could you tell me how to get to _____?**

② **Excuse me, do you know where _____ is?**

③ **Excuse me, how do I get to _____?**

🖉 常用報路句型：

① **Go straight on (street name) for (time) / (miles), ...**

② **Continue/Stay on (street name), ...**

③ **Turn left/right on (street name), ...**

🖉 常用告知位置句型：

① **It's just around the corner.**

② **It's next to (landmark).**

③ **It's across from (landmark).**

④ **It's between (landmark A) and (landmark B).**

⑤ **It's on the corner of (street A) and (street B).**

⑥ **It's on the left/right.**

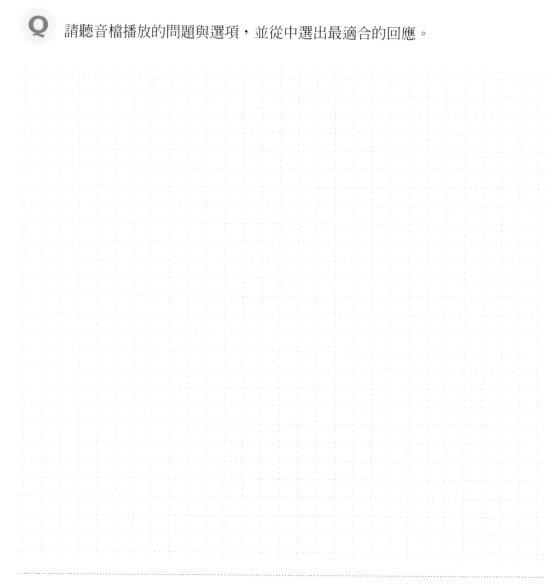

Script

Excuse me, I'm looking for the National Palace Museum.

A. Sorry, I don't know where the History Museum is.

B. Turn left at the intersection, and you'll see it.

C. Could you tell me how to get there?

Answer B

Chapter 5

Negotiation

協商交涉

在本章,你將會學習到如何看屋和協商簽約。

Situation: Sign a Rental Agreement / Lease
簽訂租約

終於,Carrie 到達了租屋處,雖然對於屋子感到滿意,但從未在海外租過房子的她,實在不知道自己應該要注意些什麼,對於屋主所提供的合約內容,又有什麼是她可以爭取的呢?

☆ 你能陪她一塊完成協商過程嗎?

Work Schedule

⊘ Check the House 檢查屋況
⊘ Negotiate the Housing Contract 協商租約

Inside + Outside 室內外

一般人租屋時，對於基本屋況和傢俱設備的狀態都會有所留意，不過往往有些重要但非天天使用到的物件卻容易被忽略。另外，除了內部的檢查，屋外環境也是需要考量的重點！建議不妨在前往租屋處前，先把該注意的要點列成清單，到時可以一一確認，這也方便自己在最後作決定時有所依據。

Step 1

室內屋況到底要檢查什麼？上至天花板，下至地板，這屋內包括的東西可多了，你認為重點的項目有哪些呢？試著列列看吧。（答案因人而異）
Up to the ceiling and down to the floor, what exactly should we check while viewing the conditions of the house inside? What are the key items you will consider? Try to list them out.

- _____
- _____
- _____

Step 2

Carrie 想來想去，還是上網看看別人都列了些什麼重點項目好了。可找到的表單內容到底問的是些什麼呢？（下表翻譯在第220頁）
With no ideas on what to check, Carrie decides to Google for suggestions. But what on earth are those questions about?

Inside / Internal	Yes	No	Note
Is it clean or freshly painted?			
Are there signs of damp or flaking paint?			
Is there any sign of loose wires?			
Are there any water leaks under the sink or in the ceiling?			
Is the carpet or floor covering in good shape?			
Are there enough electrical outlets? Do they all work?			

Inside / Internal	Yes	No	Note
Is there central heating and central air-conditioning? Do they work properly?			
Do the lights work?			
Do the windows open and close properly?			
Are there secure locks on the doors?			
Are smoke alarms fitted?			
Are kitchen appliances such as dishwashers / stove clean and working?			
Turn on the taps. Is the water pressure strong or weak?			
Does the hot water service work?			
Look under the sink and around cracks. Are there any signs of roaches or rats?			
Do repairs need to be done? Are there any broken items of furniture?			
Are there enough closets and are they large enough?			
Are there curtains?			
Do the bathroom fixtures work?			
Are there any leaks?			
Does the shower work properly?			
Is it OK for you to change the decoration like painting in the house?			

✎ Exercise 1

請根據上表問題，試著猜看看將單字填入最符合的圖片下。

- damp
- flaking paint
- loose wires
- water
- leaks under the sink
- water leaks in the ceiling
- carpet
- electrical outlets
- secure lock
- smoke alarm
- tap
- roach
- cracks
- furniture
- curtain
- bathroom fixtures
- decoration

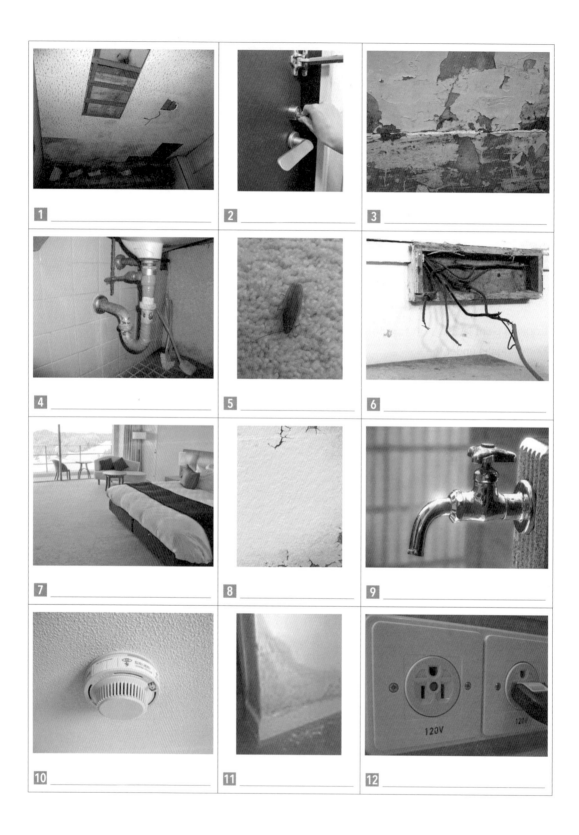

1 _____

2 _____

3 _____

4 _____

5 _____

6 _____

7 _____

8 _____

9 _____

10 _____

11 _____

12 _____

13 _____   14 _____   15 _____

Answer

1 water leaks in the ceiling 天花板漏水
2 secure locks 安全鎖
3 flaking paint 掉漆
4 water leaks under the sink 水槽下漏水
5 roach 蟑螂
6 loose wires 脫落的電線
7 carpet 地毯
8 cracks 裂縫
9 tap 水龍頭
10 smoke alarm 煙霧警報器
11 dampness 受潮
12 electrical outlets 插座
13 furniture 傢俱
14 bathroom fixtures 衛浴設備
15 decoration 裝潢

Ch 5

Step 3

檢查完室內，當然還有室外及鄰近居住環境也是要考量的重點，一樣試著列列看有哪些要項吧！（答案因人而異）

After finishing checking the interior of the house, don't forget the outside areas. Again, try to make your checklist.

■ _____

■ _____

■ _____

Step 4

關於屋外需求，Carrie 又有什麼想法呢？

What are Carrie's ideas for checking the exterior of the building?

請聽 Carrie 和 Alex 的對話，並於空格中填入適當的詞語。（下表翻譯在第221頁）

- neighbors
- street noise
- groceries
- neighborhood
- burgled
- flight path
- individual mailboxes

Alex: Hey, Carrie. I heard that you're moving to LA. So how's everything?

Carrie: Hi, Alex. It's good to hear from you. Actually, I'm still looking for the apartment. I've contacted some owners already and I'm scheduled to visit the first one tomorrow.

Alex: Sounds great. Is there anything I can help with?

Carrie: Um .... Since you mentioned it, I do have a question ....

Alex: Sure, spit it out!

Carrie: Alright. I know I need to check the condition of the house while visiting the apartment. But I only have a checklist for the inside area. So what should I check on the outside?

Alex: No worries. You've come to the right person. I can share some of my past experience.

Carrie: Superb! You're my hero.

Alex: OK, let me get my checklist and read the questions to you.

Outside / External	Yes	No	Note
Where do you pick up your mail? Are there (1) _____ ?			
Has the house ever been (2) _____ ?			
Is there too much (3) _____ or noise from nearby apartments?			
Is the house near public transport, a school or under a (4) _____ ?			
Is there a place to shop for food or (5) _____ nearby?			
Is the (6) _____ safe and clean? Will you feel comfortable walking home alone at night?			
What are the (7) _____ like?			

🔑 Key Expressions

🗝 It's good to hear from you.

表示很高興聽到對方的問候或消息，也可用於收信時。不過須注意與 hear of 區別，hear of 是「聽說」的意思。

Ex: I heard of your good news.（我聽說了你的好消息。）

🗝 schedule to (do something)

計畫或安排做某事。schedule 既可當動詞也可當名詞。

🗝 Since you mentioned it, ...

既然你提到這個……。意思是「哎呀，這可是你先提的，我才說的唷……」。

🗝 spit it out!

說吧說吧！spit 這個字本身是「吐」的意思，在這就是叫你用力把話吐出來，別拖拉了！

🗝 You've come to the right person.

「你找對人了！」這句話自賣自誇時可好用了。

Ch
5

Answer

1. individual mailboxes 獨立信箱　　2. burgled 竊盜　　3. street noise 街道噪音

4. flight path 飛航路線　　5. groceries 日用品　　6. neighborhood 鄰近地區

7. neighbors 鄰居

檢查完裡外環境，除了一些小地方外，Carrie 對這間公寓滿意極了。但到底租金合不合理？涵蓋了那些費用？不滿意的小地方是否還有可調整的空間？ Carrie 該如何在租賃契約中替自己爭取權益？

✎ Exercise 1

下面是一個超好用的價格搜尋網站。試著幫 Carrie 將以下資訊輸入，看看價錢合不合理？（答案在第101頁）

- 租屋住址：227 Olive Ave, Long Beach, CA 90802
- 價格：$ 850   ■ 類型：Studio

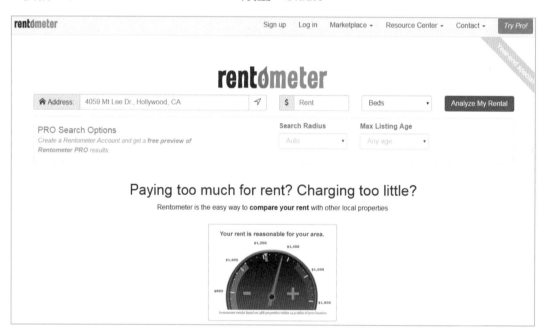

<Website> https://www.rentometer.com/

★ 另外再推薦兩個也很不錯的價格搜尋網站：

http://www.vrbo.com/   http://www.rentjungle.com/

既然價格合理，接著就要看看合約內容啦！請閱讀以下簡易合約。（翻譯在第222頁）

Rental Agreement

1. <u>Parties</u>   The parties to this agreement are

    the Landlord:

    Name: <u>Edward Murray</u>   Address: <u>213 Olive Ave</u>

    City/State/Zip: <u>Long Beach, CA 90802</u>   phone# <u>562-996-3521</u>

    the Tenant:

    Name: <u>Carrie Lee</u>   Address: <u>No. 26, Yongkang St., Da'an Dist.</u>

    City/State/Zip: <u>Taipei City 106, Taiwan (R.O.C.)</u>   phone# <u>562-724-8986</u>

2. <u>Property</u>   Landlord rents to Tenant a studio located at:

    Address: <u>227 Olive Ave</u>   City/State/Zip: <u>Long Beach, CA 90802</u>

3. The <u>term</u> of this lease shall start on: <u>1st</u> of <u>March</u>, <u>2016</u> until <u>28th</u> of <u>February</u>, <u>2017</u>.

4. The <u>rent</u> shall be <u>$850</u>/month payable in advance on the <u>1st</u> day of every month.

5. The following appliances and furniture:

    <u>Stove, oven, refrigerator, dishwasher, washing machine, dryer, air conditioner, heater, 2 closets, TV, bed</u> are included in the rental of these premises.

6. <u>Security Deposit</u>: Upon the execution of this Agreement, Tenant shall deposit with Landlord <u>One thousand and seven hundred Dollars ($1,700)</u>, as security for damage caused to the Premises during the term of the lease.

7. <u>Utilities</u> shall be paid by each party indicated below:

	LANDLORD	TENANT
Electricity		✓
Gas	✓	
Heat and Hot water		✓
Water and Sewer	✓	
Telephone		✓
Internet	✓	
Cable TV	✓	
Garbage Collection	✓	

Ch 5

8. We, the undersigned, agree to this Rental Agreement.

LANDLORD   TENANT

Edward Murray   *Carrie Lee*

02/10/2016   02/10/2016

根據上篇合約，請試著補上缺少的資訊。（答案在第101頁）

1 Landlord: _____

2 Tenant: _____

3 The address of the studio: _____

4 Monthly rent: $_____

5 Deposit: $_____

6 Starting date: _____

7 Lease term: _____

8 Pay day: _____

9 Offered appliances and furniture:

_____

10 Utilities paid by the landlord:

_____

11 Utilities paid by the tenant:

_____

🔑 Key Words

Word	Meaning
party (*n.*)	a person who is involved in a legal case or contract 當事人
agreement (*n.*)	a contract 協議；契約
tenant (*n.*)	a person who rents a house from another for a period of time 房客
property (*n.*)	a piece of land with buildings on it owned by a person or business 地產
term (*n.*)	the time or period through which something lasts 期限；期間
in advance (*phr.*)	ahead of time; beforehand 預先
premises (*n.*)	land and the buildings on it 包括附屬建築以及土地在內的房屋

execution (*n.*)	the act of doing something 執行
security (*n.*)	a guarantee 保證
damage (*n.*)	injury or harm that reduces value or usefulness 損害；毀壞
cause (*v.*)	to make something happen, to bring about 引起；導致
lease (*n.*)	a contract 相約
indicate (*v.*)	to point out 指示；標示
electricity (*n.*)	a form of energy, usually used to operate machines, lights, etc. 電力
sewer (*n.*)	an artificial conduit for carrying off waste water 下水道；汙水管
the undersigned (*n.*)	the person whose name is signed at the end of a document 簽署人

✎ Exercise 3 　🎧 Track 11

請聽 Carrie 和房東 Edward 的對話，並於空格中填入適當的詞語。（答案在第101頁）

- rent
- repainted
- $950
- utilities
- rental record
- neighborhood
- delivered
- $850
- electricity
- $1,000
- break rules
- flaking paint
- fair price
- reconsider

Edward: What do you think about the studio so far?

Carrie: It's great! I really love it.

Edward: Is everything OK? You don't have any problems with it?

Carrie: Actually, I do have a few problems.

Edward: What problems?

Carrie: There's (1)_____ on the left side of this wall.

Edward: Don't worry. I'll have the wall (2)_____ before you move in.

Carrie: Will you?

Edward: I'm very sure I will. Now, besides that, what other problems do you have?

Carrie: I also noticed that the TV is not working.

Edward: Oh, I've already bought a new one and it'll be (3)_____ next Monday.

Carrie: That's great! Alright, guess I'll take it.

Edward: I'm glad to hear you say that.

Carrie: How much would I have to pay for the (4)_____?

Edward: It's (5)_____ each month.

Carrie: That's a bit too much.

Edward: I think it's a (6)_____.

Carrie: So are all the (7) _____ included?

Edward: No, you have to pay (8) _____, heat and hot water, and the telephone.

Carrie: Wow! That means I might need to pay more than (9) _____ a month. I don't think I can afford that.

Edward: Then how much can you afford?

Carrie: What about (10) _____? I've checked the rental price in this (11) _____. I think if I need to pay part of the utilities, that should be reasonable.

Edward: Um ... I have to think about it.

Carrie: You've seen my previous (12) _____. I always paid my rent on time and never cause any trouble or (13) _____. Would you please (14) _____ my offer?

Edward: Well, that's very true. Alright, guess I can live with that.

Carrie: Cool. So we have a deal then.

🔑 Key Expressions

> 🗝 **actually = in fact / as a matter of fact**
> 「事實上」。多用於表達和前述句子相反的回應。
>
> 🗝 **I'll take it.** take 本意為「拿走」，在此則表示「我要了」、「我買了」。
>
> 🗝 **I can live with that.** 表示雖不滿意，但可勉強接受。

🔑 Key Words

Word	Meaning
so far (*phr.*)	up to now 到目前為止
repaint (*v.*)	to paint again 重新粉刷
besides (*prep.*)	in addition to 除……之外
notice (*v.*)	to pay attention to 注意
work (*v.*)	to act or operate 運作
reasonable (*a.*)	showing reason or sound judgment 合理的
previous (*a.*)	happening before now 以前的
on time (*phr.*)	according to the schedule 準時
break (*v.*)	to fail to conform to 打破；破壞
reconsider (*v.*)	to consider again 重新考慮

offer (*v.*)	something like a suggestion, proposal or ideas　提議
deal (*n.*)	a business agreement　交易；協議

....

Answer Exercise 1

Your rent is reasonable for your area.　租金很合理唷！

227 Olive Ave, Long Beach, CA 90802
Your rent is reasonable for your area.

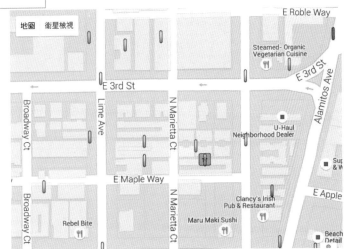

Your results are based on:

- **35** studio bedroom rentals
- ...in a **0.14** mile radius.
- Median rent: **$825**
- Average rent: **$909**
- 60% between: $698 – $1121
- 80% between: $587 – $1232

Answer Exercise 2

1 Edward Murray　　2 Carrie Lee　　3 227 Olive Ave, Long Beach, CA 90802　　4 850　　5 1,700

6 March 1, 2016　　7 1 year　　8 1st day of every month

9 Stove, oven, refrigerator, dishwasher, washing machine, dryer, air conditioner, heater, 2 closets, TV, bed

10 Gas, Water and Sewer, Internet, Cable TV, Garbage Collection

11 Electricity, Heat and Hot water, Telephone

Answer Exercise 3

(1) flaking paint　(2) repainted　(3) delivered　(4) rent　(5) $950

(6) fair price　(7) utilities　(8) electricity　(9) $1,000　(10) $850

(11) neighborhood　(12) rental record　(13) break rules　(14) reconsider

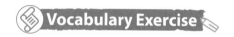

Task 1 Crossword Puzzle 填字遊戲

請根據下列英文提示，將該單字填入空格中。Hint: 可參考前面的 Key Words 表。

Across:

1. a person who is involved in a legal case or contract

3. to point out

4. the act of doing something

5. a person who rents a house from another for a period of time

7. the time or period through which something lasts

8. a piece of land with buildings on it owned by a person or business

9. an artificial conduit for carrying off waste water

10. injury or harm that reduces value or usefulness

102

12. a guarantee

13. to make something happen, to bring about

14. a form of energy, usually used to operate machines, lights, etc.

Down:

2. a contract

6. land and the buildings on it

11. a contract

Answer

1. party	2. agreement	3. indicate	4. execution	5. tenant
6. premises	7. term	8. property	9. sewer	10. damage
11. lease	12. security	13. cause	14. electricity	

Task 2 Scrambled Words 字母重組

請將左方亂序的字母重組成有意義的單字。

1 lalcuaty _____

2 arnietp _____

3 eesbids _____

4 oicent _____

5 srbaoaeenl _____

6 iovpesru _____

7 ebrka _____

8 recrsdione _____

9 fefro _____

10 dlae _____

Answer

1 actually	2 repaint	3 besides	4 notice	5 reasonable
6 previous	7 break	8 reconsider	9 offer	10 deal

CHAPTER SUMMARY

Prepare a checklist for the internal and external areas of the buliding. Mark down the problems you see.

準備檢查屋內和屋外環境狀況的清單。把問題記錄下來。

↓

Some important items to check in the inside area:

屋內重要檢查項目有：

① **water leaks** 漏水　② **dampness** 受潮　　③ **secure locks** 安全鎖

④ **flaking paint** 掉漆　⑤ **loose wires** 脫落的電線　⑥ **smoke alarm** 煙霧警報器

⑦ **appliances and furniture** 傢俱設備

↓

Some important items to check in the outside area:

屋外重要檢查項目有：

① **individual mailboxes** 獨立信箱　　　　　② **burglary** 竊盜

③ **street noise** 街道噪音　④ **flight path** 飛航路線　⑤ **grocery store** 雜貨店

⑥ **neighborhood** 鄰近地區　⑦ **neighbors** 鄰居

↓

Check the fair market rents online.

上網查詢該地區的合理市場價格。

★ 推薦三個查詢好站：

1. https://www.rentometer.com/

2. http://www.vrbo.com/

3. http://www.rentjungle.com/

↓

Understand the terms in the rental agreement.

了解合約內容，像是：

① **party** 當事人　　② **property** 物產　　③ **term** 期限　　④ **rent** 租金

⑤ **appliances and furniture** 傢俱設備　　⑥ **security deposit** 保證金

⑦ **utilities** 水電雜費

Ask for repairs if needed. And try to negotiate the rent.

如果有必要的話，要求修復，以及別忘了試試看講價。

★ 若是要更有保障，別忘了請房東將答應修復的地方白紙黑字寫下來。另外，想壓低租金，
　要記得多說說自己的優良租屋紀錄或是特點，替自己加分喔！

Q 請根據這篇文章，回答下列兩個問題。

Rental property repair responsibility

When facing home repairs, you might not have time to argue with your landlord or tenant about the repair bill, but definitely you do not want to pay for something that is not your responsibility. Therefore, knowing the mutual rights and responsibilities is the best way to reduce dispute expenses and time.

Basically, if repairs come from wear and tear over time, a landlord is responsible for the payment. However, if damage occurs as a consequence of human error, the repair cost should be paid by the tenant. For example, when a faucet breaks due to corrosion over time, the landlord should take the responsibility to pay for the repairs. On the other hand, if the break arises from certain kind of wrong operation, then the tenant should be responsible for the damage.

Q1.

What is the article mainly about?

(A) The responsibility of house owners

(B) The responsibility of contractors

(C) The responsibility of renters and occupants

(D) The responsibility of real estate agents

Q2.

Where would the article most likely be found?

(A) In a home improvement magazine

(B) In a newspaper advertisement

(C) In a home repair shop

(D) In a policy guide to rental housing

Answer 1. C   2. D

Chapter 6

Banking
銀行業務

在本章，你將會學習到如何開戶和存提款。

Situation: Go to a Bank 去銀行

談好了租約，付好了押金，但 Carrie 身上還剩了許多錢呢。在尚未搬入新家前，Carrie 決定還是先到銀行開戶，把錢都存進去比較安心。可一到了櫃台，面對行員，Carrie 卻不知該如何說明來意。

☆ 你能陪她一塊完成開戶嗎？

Work Schedule

⊘ Open an Account 開戶
⊘ Deposit and Withdraw Money 存提款

TASK 1　Open an Account

Saving or Checking Account 儲蓄戶或活期戶

如同在台灣一樣，要在銀行開戶，不會只有一種選擇。不過對外國人來說，若是不涉及投資，最常見的大概就是儲蓄戶和活期戶兩種。各家銀行的利率和優惠不同，要選到最好的，恐怕不是短期就可以掌握的。對於初來乍到的外國人而言，一般還是建議選擇離自己住家，或是工作讀書場所近的銀行為首選唷！

Step 1

到銀行開戶絕不是兩手空空就可以進行的。想想看有什麼要事先準備的呢？勾選要用的文件吧。

We cannot open an account empty-handed. What should we prepare beforehand? Check the documents you think are required.

☐ Passport   ☐ Documentation of Your Address

☐ ID   ☐ Initial Deposit

☐ Driver's License   ☐ Photograph

☐ Stamp   ☐ Proof of Employment

☐ Social Security Number   ☐ Student ID

Answer

☑ Passport 護照 / ID 身分證 / Driver's License 駕照 → 擇一即可

☐ Stamp 印章 → 國外並不使用印鑑

☑ Social Security Number 社會安全碼 → 對外國人來說，一般除非有工作，否則並不會擁有。

  ★ 社會安全碼係由美國政府核發，類似台灣的身分證字號，於報稅、找工作、申請帳戶和醫療等時使用。

☑ Documentation of Your Address 住址證明 → 可以用各類帳單來證明

☑ Initial Deposit 起存額 → 通常開戶都須先存入一筆最低金額

☐ Photograph 照片 → 現在銀行大多都可以直接照相了

☑ Proof of Employment 工作證明 / Student ID 學生證 → 擇一即可

Step 2

帶好了東西，接著開戶時就要決定好，到底是要開儲蓄戶還是活期戶。但這兩種帳戶到底有什麼差別？

Now we're ready to open an account. But which type of bank account is best for our needs, a savings account or a checking account?

✏️ Exercise 1

請閱讀以下摘錄自 Wells Fargo Bank 網站，關於儲蓄戶 (savings account) 或活期戶 (checking account) 的資訊。（翻譯在第225頁）

Checking account: A checking account offers easy access to your money for your daily transactional needs and helps keep your cash secure. Customers can use a debit card or checks to make purchases or pay bills. Accounts may have different options or packages to help waive certain monthly service fees.

Savings account: A savings account allows you to accumulate interest on funds you've saved for future needs. Interest rates can be compounded on a daily, weekly, monthly, or annual basis. Savings accounts vary by monthly service fees, interest rates, method used to calculate interest, and minimum opening deposit.

<Website> https://www.wellsfargo.com/financial-education/basic-finances/manage-money/options/bank-account-types/

註 兩種帳戶的敘述雖然看起來有點長，不過掌握住關鍵第一句就差不多可以懂啦。

看完了有關帳戶的特性說明，你答得出下面各是在問哪種帳戶嗎？

1 Which one can help you make more money?
2 Which one can help you get your money easily for routine banking activities?

....

Answer

1 Savings account   2 Checking account

Step 3

對 Carrie 來說，她只是短期居留，開戶主要當然是應付日常花費，你覺得她該開什麼帳戶呢？

Carrie isn't going to stay long in the States. For her, the account is mainly for her daily expense. What kind of account do you think she needs?

Answer

Checking account

Step 4

決定好了開什麼戶之後，接著 Carrie 得把自己帶來的旅行支票先給存進去。可旅支該怎麼兌現呢？

購買時立即簽
用時再複簽

After deciding the type of account she is going to open, Carrie needs to cash and deposit her traveler's checks. How does she do it?

✏ Exercise 2

你可以將下列兌換旅支的指示按順序排出嗎？（答案和翻譯在第111頁）

_____ (a) Write the date in the upper right corner of the check.

___1___ (b) Go to a bank that accepts travelers checks and exchange them for US dollars.

_____ (c) Pay the commission fees if required.

_____ (d) Write the name of the bank on the "pay this check to the order of" line.

_____ (e) Give the check to the bank teller along with your passport.

_____ (f) Sign your name in the lower left corner of the check. Make sure the bank teller watches as you sign. Your signature should match the original signature in the upper left of the check.

 **Key Words**

Word	Meaning
access (*n.*)	the ability to approach, use or get something 接近；進入
transactional (*a.*)	having business with other people 交易的
debit card (*n.*)	a card used to withdraw cash or buy things for which the payment is directly taken from a bank account. 金融卡；提款卡；現金卡（可直接於商店刷卡消費）
check/cheque (*n.*)	a written order directing a bank to pay money 支票
purchase (*n.*)	the act of buying 購買
waive (*v.*)	to refrain from applying a rule 免於；放棄
allow (*v.*)	to let do or happen 允許
interest (*n.*)	the profit you get from the money you invest 利息
compound (*v.*)	to pay interest on the money you saved at the beginning and the interest you've already earned 複利
basis (*n.*)	anything on which something is based 基礎
minimum (*n.*)	the lowest possible amount 最小量
accept (*v.*)	to take or receive 接受
commission fee (*n.*)	a fee paid to an agent for doing business 手續費
require (*v.*)	to need 需要
bank teller (*n.*)	a person who deals with customers over the counter in a bank 銀行櫃員
original (*a.*)	happening first or the beginning of something 最初的；原始的
signature (*n.*)	a person's name written by himself or herself 簽名

Ch 6

Answer

__2__ (a) 於旅支右上方寫上兌換日期

__1__ (b) 前往可以接受你旅支的銀行兌換美金

__6__ (c) 根據要求支付手續費

__3__ (d) 在中間 "pay this check to the order of"（付給誰）寫下兌換銀行名

__5__ (e) 將旅支和護照一起交給行員

__4__ (f) 於左下方簽名，這必須由行員看著你簽名，並且簽名要和左上方原先簽過的名一樣。

請聽 Carrie 和行員的對話，並於空格中填入適當的詞語。

- open an account
- passport
- interest rate
- 6
- checking account
- savings account
- student ID
- 3,000
- 50
- initial deposit

Bank teller: Good morning Miss, what can I do for you today?

Carrie: I'd like to (1) _____.

Bank teller: Certainly. What kind of account would you like to open? Checking or savings?

Carrie: Uh ... what's the difference between the two?

Bank teller: The (2) _____ offers easy access to your money. That is, you can withdraw your money any time. But the account doesn't pay you any interest. As for the (3) _____, the current (4) _____ is 2.35% for a one-year deposit, and 3.5% for a three-year deposit. However, you are only allowed to withdraw money no more than (5) _____ times a month.

Carrie: Oh, I see. Well, I'm here for studying. So guess I'll go for the checking account.

Bank teller: Sure, so how much would you like to deposit today? Our (6) _____ is $(7) _____.

Carrie: I'll be depositing $(8) _____.

Bank teller: OK, please fill out this form and give me your (9) _____ and (10) _____. I'll set up your account right away.

Answer

(1) open an account　(2) checking account　(3) savings account　(4) interest rate　(5) 6

(6) initial deposit　(7) 50　(8) 3,000　(9) passport　(10) student ID

🔑 Key Expressions

🔖 **Certainly. = Sure. = Of course. = No problem. = Definitely. = Absolutely.**

其實就是在說 "yes"，回應對方，表示「當然」、「好的」。

🔖 **That is = That is to say**

即「也就是說」的意思。

🔖 **as for + sb or sth**

至於；說到……。用來引出另一個主題，和前述內容形成對比。

🔖 **no more than**

不超過；只有，和 only 差不多。

🔖 **go for + sth**

在此表「選擇」某物。

★ 也常聽到人說 "Go for it!"，用來鼓勵對方全力以赴、努力爭取。

🔖 **I'll be depositing**

在此因為是表示即將要發生的動作，強調動作進行，所以使用了未來進行式，而非簡單式。

🔖 **fill out**

填寫。也可以用 fill in，後面大多接 form（表格）。

🔑 Key Words

Word	Meaning
withdraw (v.)	to take back, to remove 取回；提取
current (a.)	happening or existing now 現行的；當前的

TASK 2 Withdraw Money

Checkbook and Debit Card 支票本和提款卡

開完戶了！ Carrie 拿到了一本支票本和一張金融卡。但是該怎麼使用它們呢？

✎ Exercise 1

在 ATM 使用金融卡提款，基本上全世界的方式都差不多。試著將下面的提款步驟
按順序排列好吧！（答案和翻譯在第116頁）

_____ (a) Choose whether you wish to do another transaction; select Yes or No.

_____ (b) Take out the cash.

_____ (c) Choose "checking account" or "savings account".

_____ (d) Enter the amount you wish to withdraw.

_____ (e) Take your receipt.

_____ (f) Wait for the system to count your money and dispense it through the slot.

___1___ (g) Find an ATM machine.

_____ (h) Enter your PIN (4-8 digit personal identification number), and then press "Enter."

_____ (i) Select a transaction: Withdrawal.

_____ (j) Choose whether you want a receipt; select Yes or No.

_____ (k) Insert your ATM/Debit Card into the machine or swipe it.

✎ Exercise 2

進行提款時，Carrie 發現 ATM 除了提款之外，還有其他交易功能，你知道的有哪
些呢？動動腦列出來吧！（答案各家銀行機器不一）

■ _____   ■ _____

■ _____   ■ _____

■ _____   ■ _____

✐ Exercise 3

下列左邊是關於 ATM 交易功能的字詞，試著透過部分你知道的單字，連連看中文是什麼意思吧！

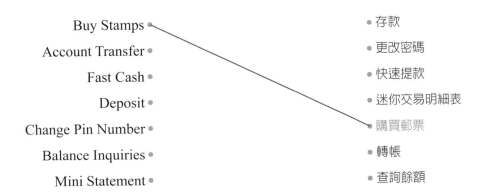

Buy Stamps •
Account Transfer •
Fast Cash •
Deposit •
Change Pin Number •
Balance Inquiries •
Mini Statement •

• 存款
• 更改密碼
• 快速提款
• 迷你交易明細表
• 購買郵票
• 轉帳
• 查詢餘額

✐ Exercise 4

雖然 debit card 也可當作信用卡一樣，使用於一般店家，可 Carrie 要付的押金和房租，房東不接收刷卡。為了不讓宵小覬覦現款，Carrie 決定開支票。但支票上的這些項目各代表什麼呢？根據圖片上的訊息試著猜猜看吧！

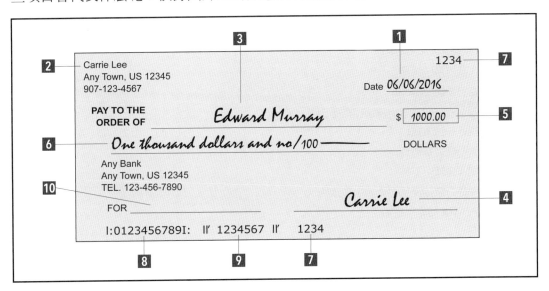

1	_____	2	_____
3	_____	4	_____
5	_____	6	_____

Ch 6

115

7 Check number（本張支票號碼）

8 Routing number（路由代碼，用於確認金融機構，匯款時需要）

9 Account number（帳戶號碼）

10 _____

Answer Exercise 1

  9 (a) 選擇是否要進行其他交易，是或否。

  8 (b) 取走現金

  5 (c) 選擇儲蓄戶或活期戶

  6 (d) 輸入欲提取的金額

 11 (e) 取走交易明細表

  7 (f) 等候系統數鈔完畢後由出口處送出

  1 (g) 先找好一台 ATM

  3 (h) 輸入密碼後按確認

  4 (i) 選擇「提款」交易

 10 (j) 選擇是否需要交易明細表，是或否。

  2 (k) 插入 ATM 提款卡或刷卡

Answer Exercise 3

Account Transfer = 轉帳　　　　　Fast Cash = 快速提款（有固定的金額選項可選）

Deposit = 存款　　　　　　　　　Change Pin Number = 更改密碼

Balance Inquiries = 查詢餘額　　　Mini Statement = 迷你交易明細表（提供最近十次的交易紀錄）

Answer Exercise 4

① 填寫日期　　　② 帳戶持有人資料　　　③ 受款人　　　④ 付款人簽名

⑤ 支付金額（數字表示）　　⑥ 支付金額（文字表示）　　⑩ 支票用途（可寫可不寫）

Vocabulary Exercise

Task 1 Crossword Puzzle 填字遊戲

請根據下列英文提示，將該單字填入空格中。Hint: 可參考前面的 Key Words 表。

Ch 6

Across:

4. to take or receive

6. the ability to approach, use or get something

7. the lowest possible amount

9. happening first or the beginning of something

10. a written order directing a bank to pay money

11. the profit you get from the money you invest

13. happening or existing now

14. to let do or happen

16. the act of buying

Down:

1. having business with other people

2. anything on which something is based

3. to need

5. a person's name written by himself or herself

8. to take back, to remove

12. to pay interest on the money you saved at the beginning and the interest you've already earned

15. to refrain from applying a rule

Answer

1. transactional	2. basis	3. require	4. accept
5. signature	6. access	7. minimum	8. withdraw
9. original	10. check	11. interest	12. compound
13. current	14. allow	15. waive	16. purchase

Task 2 Word Search 找字

請於下表中找出以下這些詞彙。Hint: 答案有可能是右到左或下到上排列。

- ACCEPT
- ACCESS
- ACCUMULATE
- ALLOW
- ANNUAL
- BASIS
- CHECK
- COMPOUND
- CURRENT
- EXCHANGE
- FUND
- INTEREST
- MINIMUM
- ORIGINAL
- PURCHASE
- REQUIRE
- SIGNATURE
- TRANSACTIONAL
- WAIVE
- WITHDRAW

E	G	N	A	H	C	X	E	C	E	O	M	M	I	S
R	E	Q	U	I	R	E	S	I	O	V	N	F	E	E
R	Z	B	H	X	W	T	I	J	A	Z	I	V	R	U
V	E	I	C	N	K	T	W	I	V	T	L	A	H	Q
X	K	H	I	F	S	B	S	S	E	C	C	A	W	I
P	I	P	S	I	G	N	A	T	U	R	E	R	X	C
L	A	N	O	I	T	C	A	S	N	A	R	T	P	O
S	O	C	T	F	M	L	H	L	V	T	R	U	W	M
T	W	R	U	E	U	U	A	E	P	L	R	S	A	P
R	N	N	I	M	R	U	M	E	C	C	T	I	R	O
B	D	E	U	G	N	E	C	I	H	K	P	S	D	U
D	W	C	R	N	I	C	S	A	N	N	B	A	H	N
M	C	V	A	R	A	N	S	T	E	I	A	B	T	D
A	A	C	S	P	U	E	A	F	A	N	M	L	I	W
W	O	L	L	A	V	C	J	L	Q	O	B	R	W	R

Ch
6

Answer

E	G	N	A	H	C	X	E	C	E	O	M	M	I	S
R	E	Q	U	I	R	E	S	I	O	V	N	F	E	E
R	Z	B	H	X	W	T	I	J	A	Z	I	V	R	U
V	E	I	C	N	K	T	W	I	V	T	L	A	H	Q
X	K	H	I	F	S	B	S	S	E	C	C	A	W	I
P	I	P	S	I	G	N	A	T	U	R	E	R	X	C
L	A	N	O	I	T	C	A	S	N	A	R	T	P	O
S	O	C	T	F	M	L	H	L	V	T	R	U	W	M
T	W	R	U	E	U	U	A	E	P	L	R	S	A	P
R	N	N	I	M	R	U	M	E	C	C	T	I	R	O
B	D	E	U	G	N	E	C	I	H	K	P	S	D	U
D	W	C	R	N	I	C	S	A	N	N	B	A	H	N
M	C	V	A	R	A	N	S	T	E	I	A	B	T	D
A	A	C	S	P	U	E	A	F	A	N	M	L	I	W
W	O	L	L	A	V	C	J	L	Q	O	B	R	W	R

CHAPTER SUMMARY

Prepare the required documents for opening an account.
準備好開戶需要的文件。

 一般外國人須準備：

① **Passport** 護照

② **Documentation of Your Address** 住址證明

③ **Initial Deposit** 起存額

④ **Proof of Employment** 工作證明 / **Student ID** 學生證 → 擇一即可

↓

Choose to open a savings or checking account, or maybe both.
選擇開儲蓄戶或支票（活期）戶，也可兩者都開。

↓

Cash traveler' checks. 兌換旅支。

★ 別忘了攜帶護照前往。

↓

Withdraw money from an ATM. 從 ATM 提款。

★ 一般提款都會扣交易手續費，可於開戶前先問清楚，幫助自己省錢喔！

↓

Write a check. 寫支票。

★ 寫金額的時候要小心，以免他人竄改。

Q 請聽音檔播放的問題與選項，並從中選出最適合的回應。

Script

I'd like to open a checking account.

A. You can check in here.

B. What's your account number?

C. Please fill out these forms first.

Answer C

Chapter 7

Ordering Food
點餐

在本章，你將會學習到如何點餐和結帳。

Situation: At a Restaurant 在餐廳

辦完了銀行事務後，Carrie 一看也快到了午餐時刻，摸著發餓的肚皮，Carrie 想要好好找間餐廳大吃一頓。可看著侍者遞給她的菜單，Carrie 卻不知該如何開始點起。

☆ 你能陪她一塊完成點餐嗎？

Work Schedule

⊘ Read the Menu and Order Food 看菜單點餐

⊘ Wrap Up and Pay the Bill 打包和結帳

和速食店不同，稍正式的西餐廳菜單往往花樣多，可沒辦法讓顧客看圖點餐。且因少有套餐型式，所以別以爲點了主菜後，就會送上一堆附餐唷！此外須注意的是，一般美國餐廳提供的份量都很多，即便光點個沙拉或湯都可能讓你很飽，因此可別一下點太多了。若是初來乍到，建議還是請侍者直接推薦吧！

Step 1

想一想，若是到西餐廳用餐，菜單上會有哪些餐點種類呢？試著列列看。

How many course sections can you see in a steak restaurant's menu? List as many as you can.

- Appetizers / Starters 前菜
- _____
- _____
- _____
- _____
- _____

Answer

其他還有：

湯 Soups、沙拉 Salads、主菜 Entrées (= Main courses)、甜點 Desserts、飲料 Beverages 等

Step 2

知道了餐點種類，就能依據自己需求快速聚焦，對其下的餐點做選擇。可有些餐廳會爲了表現創意和特殊性，取些花俏的名字，這時可以參考餐點名稱下的說明，大致了解食材跟做法。

Now you can quickly search the menu and choose the dishes you like. However, some restaurants may use fancy names for the dishes. In that case, you may refer to the simple explanations below them.

✏ Exercise 1

下列是西餐廳裡各類常見的品項，你知道它們各應歸在哪
一類底下嗎？試著上網搜尋圖片後歸類吧。

1. Appetizers   2. Soups
3. Desserts   4. Beverages

_____ Banana Pudding

_____ Bottled Water

_____ Crab Cakes with Cream

_____ Nachos

_____ Lemon Cheesecake

_____ Stuffed Mushrooms

_____ Vanilla Crème Brûlée

_____ French Onion Soup

__4__ Coffee

_____ Orange Juice

_____ Baked Potato Skins

_____ Red Velvet Brownies

_____ Strawberry Tart

_____ Clam Chowder

_____ Pumpkin Cupcakes

_____ Black Tea

_____ Carrot Cake

_____ Potato Soup

_____ Spicy Black Bean Soup

_____ Baked Buffalo Chicken Wings

_____ Chicken Noodle Soup

_____ Coke

Ch
7

....

Answer

__3__ Banana Pudding 香蕉布丁

__4__ Bottled Water 瓶裝水

__1__ Crab Cakes with Cream 奶油蟹肉餅

__1__ Nachos 墨西哥辣肉醬起司烤玉米片

__3__ Lemon Cheesecake 檸檬起司蛋糕

__1__ Stuffed Mushrooms 焗釀蘑菇

__3__ Vanilla Crème Brûlée 香草布蕾

__2__ French Onion Soup 法式洋蔥湯

__4__ Coffee 咖啡

__4__ Orange Juice 柳橙汁

__1__ Baked Potato Skins 烤馬鈴薯皮

__3__ Red Velvet Brownies 紅絲絨布朗尼

__3__ Strawberry Tart 草莓塔

__2__ Clam Chowder 蛤蠣巧達湯

__3__ Pumpkin Cupcakes 南瓜杯子蛋糕

__4__ Black Tea 紅茶

__3__ Carrot Cake 胡蘿蔔蛋糕

__2__ Potato Soup 馬鈴薯湯

__2__ Spicy Black Bean Soup 辣黑豆湯

__1__ Baked Buffalo Chicken Wings 烤雞翅

__2__ Chicken Noodle Soup 雞湯麵

__4__ Coke 可樂

Step 3

下列提供幾種常見的沙拉。

Following are examples of common salads.

Salads:

Seafood Salad 海鮮沙拉、Caesar Salad 凱薩沙拉、Chef Salad 主廚沙拉、Fruit Salad 水果沙拉、Garden Salad 田園沙拉 等

✏ Exercise 2

說到沙拉，當然不能不知道沙拉醬的選擇，你知道有哪些嗎？以下是幾種常見的沙拉醬，試著連連看吧。

Caesar Salad Dressing •   • 希臘醬

Italian Oil and Vinegar Salad Dressing •   • 凱薩醬

Thousand Island Salad Dressing •   • 藍起司醬

Blue Cheese Salad Dressing •   • 覆盆子醋醬

Honey Mustard Salad Dressing •   • 義大利油醋醬

Ranch Salad Dressing •   • 蜂蜜芥末醬

Greek Salad Dressing •   • 田園醬

French Salad Dressing •   • 法式醬

Balsamic Vinaigrette Salad Dressing •   • 千島醬

Raspberry Vinaigrette Salad Dressing •   • 義大利陳年葡萄醋醬

Answer

Italian Oil and Vinegar Salad Dressing = 義大利油醋醬

Thousand Island Salad Dressing = 千島醬

Blue Cheese Salad Dressing = 藍起司醬

Honey Mustard Salad Dressing = 蜂蜜芥末醬

Ranch Salad Dressing = 田園醬

Greek Salad Dressing = 希臘醬

French Salad Dressing = 法式醬

Balsamic Vinaigrette Salad Dressing = 義大利陳年葡萄醋醬

Raspberry Vinaigrette Salad Dressing = 覆盆子醋醬

Step 4

下列提供幾種常見的牛排，多以牛的部位做區分。大家都知道若要吃牛排，可是要考量熟度，你知道一般分成哪些呢？

Below are some popular steak choices, distinguished by the cuts of steak. We know that we can ask for a steak to be cooked to different degrees of doneness. So how many common choices are there?

Steak:

Rib Eye steak 肋眼牛排

New York Strip steak 紐約客牛排

Beef Tenderloin 牛里脊肉

T-bone steak 丁骨牛排

Flank steak 側腹牛排

Sirloin steak 沙朗牛排

Prime Rib 頂級肋眼

Skirt steak 側腹橫肌牛排

Filet Mignon 菲力牛排

Porterhouse steak 上等腰肉牛排

Answer

rare = 1 分熟　　medium rare = 3 分熟　　medium = 5 分熟　　medium well = 7 分熟　　well done = 全熟

✎ Exercise 3　🎧 **Track 14**

請聽 Carrie 和服務生的對話，並於空格中填入適當的詞語。

■ brownie　　　　　■ French fries　　　　■ pudding　　　　　■ clam chowder
■ crab cakes　　　　■ orange juice　　　　■ rib eye

Server: Hi, good afternoon. I will be your server today. Can I get you a drink?

Carrie: Yes, I would like a glass of (1) _____ with ice.

Server: OK. I will be right back with your drink.

·······························(three minutes later)·······························

Server: Here is your orange juice. So are you ready to order, or do you need a couple more minutes?

Carrie: I'm ready. I think I'll start with the (2) _____ with cream and the (3) _____ .

Server: Good choices. And what would you like for a main course?

Carrie: Well, I'm not quite sure. What's good here?

Server: I recommend you try the rib eye. It's very popular.

Carrie: Alright, I'll have the (4) _____ then.

Server: Certainly. And how would you like your steak?

Carrie: Medium well, please.

Server: The rib eye is served with a choice of mashed potatoes, baked potatoes, or French fries. Which would you prefer?

Carrie: I'll take the (5) _____ .

Server: OK, so that's one crab cakes with cream, one clam chowder, and one rib eye with French fries. Your food will be here shortly.

···················· (an hour later) ····················

Server: How was everything?

Carrie: Delicious! I really enjoyed them.

Server: Would you like anything for dessert?

Carrie: Yes. Can I have the dessert menu please?

Server: Here you go.

Carrie: The red velvet brownie and the banana pudding both look yummy.

Server: They both are good. But if you like something sweeter, you might want to try the (6) _____ .

Carrie: Oh, I'm not a fan of sugar. Maybe I'll try the (7) _____ instead.

Server: No problem.

Answer

(1) orange juice   (2) crab cakes   (3) clam chowder   (4) rib eye   (5) French fries

(6) brownie   (7) pudding

🔑 Key Expressions

- **would like = want** 為比較正式有禮貌的用法。

- **a couple of** couple 本來是指「一雙」、「一對」，所以 a couple of 有「約略為二」的意思，多於一個，但並非一定是兩個。後接複數名詞，如 a couple of minutes（約兩分鐘）。而口語中，常會將 a couple of 加上 more 一起使用，但省略 of，變成如對話中的 a couple more minutes（再幾分鐘）。

- **How would you like you steak?** 在這用 how，表示的是程度和方法，也就是詢問你想如何烹煮你的牛排。

- **take** 在這和 "have" 意思相同，都有拿走某選項的意思。

  若是買衣服時也可以說：I'll take the blue one.（我要 拿走 / 買走 藍色的。）

- **Here you go. = Here you are.** 拿去；給你。別人遞物品給自己時也常會使用。

- **I'm not a fan of sugar.** 我不嗜吃甜。

  Fan 可作「愛好者」解，而 baseball fan 當然就是指棒球迷。

🔑 Key Words

Word	Meaning
main course (*n.*)	the biggest or most important part of a meal 主菜
quite (*adv.*)	very, really 相當；頗
recommend (*v.*)	to say that something is good and worth experiencing 推薦
popular (*a.*)	widely liked by many people 受歡迎的
mashed potatoes (*n.*)	potatoes that have been boiled and mashed 馬鈴薯泥
prefer (*v.*)	like one thing better than another or others 更偏愛
shortly (*adv.*)	in a short time, soon 馬上；立刻
delicious (*a.*)	very pleasant to the taste 美味的
yummy (*a.*)	very pleasant to the taste 美味的
instead (*adv.*)	in place of someone or something 替代
tip (*n.*)	a small amount of money given directly to someone for performing a service or task 小費

終於，Carrie 覺得自己撐得再也吃不下了。看看時間也該走了，Carrie 叫來服務生準備結帳，但拿到帳單的 Carrie 到底該付多少錢呢？

```
                TOP Steakhouse
               6600 E. First St.
             Long Beach, CA 90803

                 Guest Check
           Thank you for visiting TOP
      -------------------------------------
              TABLE: 45 - 1 Guest
            Your Server was [Jeff]
            8/31/2016  9:48:16 PM
            Sequence #: 0000230
               ID #: 0249399
      -------------------------------------
       ITEM                  QTY    PRICE
      -------------------------------------
       Orange Juice           1     $3.50
       Crab Cakes             1     $9.25
       Clam Chowder           1     $4.75
       Rib Eye                1    $17.00
       Pudding                1     $6.00
      -------------------------------------
                Subtotal            $40.50
                Tax                  $4.05
      -------------------------------------
                Grand Total         $44.55
                Amount Due          $44.55
      -------------------------------------
              See You Again Soon!
                 Guest Check
```

✏️ Exercise 1

根據上面的收據，你可以猜出它們的意思嗎？試著連連看吧！

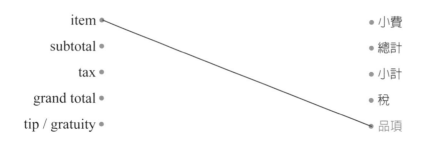

item ●   ● 小費

subtotal ●   ● 總計

tax ●   ● 小計

grand total ●   ● 稅

tip / gratuity ●   ● 品項

✐ Exercise 2

Tipping etiquette

How much should we tip at a restaurant? It depends on various factors, such as the type of restaurant, the size of your party, the kinds of services provided, and the quality of the service.

In the United States, the generally accepted value is 10-20% of the total bill before taxes: 20% for excellent service, 15% for average service, and 10% for poor service.

However, many restaurants will automatically add a gratuity to the bill for parties over six. So don't forget to check if the tip is already included in the bill!

看了上面介紹小費禮儀的短文之後，你知道對服務很滿意的 Carrie 該給多少小費嗎？（翻譯在第227頁）

✐ Exercise 3   Track 15

以下是在餐廳要求打包時常用的字詞，請試著填入適當的空格內。

■ take ... home　　　　■ to-go box / doggy bag (informal)　　　　■ wrap ... up

Server: Hi, is everything OK?

Carrie: Yes, it was really delicious, but I'm full. I'd like to (1)＿＿＿＿＿ the rest of it (1)＿＿＿＿＿. Can I get a (2)＿＿＿＿＿ please?

Server: Oh, no worries. I will (3)＿＿＿＿＿ it (3)＿＿＿＿＿ for you.

Carrie: Great, thanks.

Answer Exercise 1

subtotal = 小計　　　tax = 稅　　　grand total = 總計　　　tip / gratuity = 小費

Answer Exercise 2

給予 20% 的小費

Subtotal: $40.50　　　Tip: $40.50 * (0.2) = $8.1

不是刷卡的話，小費可以直接留在桌上喔！

Answer Exercise 3

(1) take ... home　　　(2) to-go box　　　(3) wrap ... up

Task 1 Crossword Puzzle 填字遊戲

請根據下列英文提示，將該單字填入空格中。Hint: 可參考前面的 Key Words 表。

Across:

3. in place of someone or something

5. very

6. widely liked by many people

7. very pleasant to the taste

8. like one thing better than another or others

Down:

1. a small amount of money given directly to someone for performing a service or task

2. to say that something is good and worth experiencing

4. in a short time

Answer

1. tip   2. recommend   3. instead   4. shortly

5. quite   6. popular   7. delicious   8. prefer

132

Task 2 Scrambled Words 字母重組

請將左方亂序的字母重組成有意義的單字。

1 qtiue _____

2 mmedrnoec _____

3 iielcudso _____

4 osrtylh _____

5 pti _____

6 pulropa _____

7 rrefep _____

8 xat _____

9 isentda _____

10 yuymm _____

11 ultsotba _____

12 tmei _____

Ch
7

....

CHAPTER SUMMARY

Look for the course section based on your needs, and turn to that section.
根據你的需求找尋餐點種類，並翻至該頁。

- 前菜 **Appetizers / Starters**
- 湯 **Soups**
- 沙拉 **Salads**
- 甜點 **Desserts**
- 主菜 **Entrées (= Main courses)**
- 飲料 **Beverages**

Get to know some common dishes in each section.
了解幾種各類常見餐點。

★ 若看不懂餐點是什麼的話，可參考其名稱下的說明，大致了解食材和做法。

Know your favorite of salad dressings and how you like your steak cooked.
知道沙拉醬和牛排熟度的選擇。

- **rare** 1 分熟
- **medium rare** 3 分熟
- **medium** 5 分熟
- **medium well** 7 分熟
- **well done** 全熟

Tip your server 10-20 % of the total bill before taxes.
給予侍者稅前總消費額 10-20% 的小費。

- **20% for excellent service**
- **15% for average service**
- **10% for poor service**

Ask the server to wrap up your leftovers.
要求打包。

Q 請為下列空格選出最合適的字詞。

Maintaining proper _____ during business meetings encourages respect and cooperation among participants, which helps the meeting be more effective and efficient.

(A) appropriateness

(B) essence

(C) complexity

(D) etiquette

Answer D

Chapter 8

Shopping
購物

在本章，你將會學習到如何看懂特價訊息及詢問退換貨。

Situation: At a Shopping Mall 在購物中心

終於搬好了家，Carrie 決定趁著學校還沒開學，替自己添購些衣物。一到了購物中心發現四處都在打折，真是太好了！可這各式不同的特價資訊，到底能讓 Carrie 撿到什麼便宜呢？

☆ 你能陪她一塊完成採購嗎？

Work Schedule

⊘ Read Advertisements 看懂特價廣告
⊘ Enquire about the Return Policy 詢問退換貨規定

TASK 1 Read Advertisements

In the Store 在店內

特價期間通常都是隨著季節更換或特定節日而來,折扣低到二、三折都有。特價資訊往往在店外就能看到,但入內卻不見得全都是折扣商品,大多會分成新品和過季折扣區,而即便是折扣區,折扣也可能不盡相同,因此挑選時可得注意看清楚喔!

Step 1

特價廣告隨店家各異,不過基本的組成要素大致相同。看看這兩個廣告範例,你知道下面這些要素各代表什麼意思嗎?

Sale ads might vary from one to another, but the basic elements are mostly the same. After reading the two ads below, can you figure out the meaning of the following phrases?

Women's Sneakers
Brand ABC
Sale: $29.99
Was: $99.99
Orig: $109.99
Save: 73%

Women's Sneakers
Brand ABC
Sale: $29.99
Was: $99.99
Orig: $109.99
Save: 73%

Women's Sneakers
Brand ABC
Sale: $29.99
Was: $99.99
Orig: $109.99
Save: 73%

Snowman Mall

TK STYLE
Sportswear

SPRING
SALE
up to 60% off
on selected items

March 25 till midnight
March 26 & 27 regular hours

A 折數   B 原價   C 店名   D 折扣期   E 品項   F 特價

1 item _____
2 original price _____
3 sale price / discounted price _____

4 discount percentage _____
5 sale time _____
6 store name _____

....

Answer

1 E   2 B   3 F   4 A   5 D   6 C

Step 2

除了廣告上概略的特價資訊外，走進店家還得注意其細分的不同特價標示。
Besides the sale information in ads or on posters, customers should also pay attention to the various sale signs in the store.

✏ Exercise 1

根據下列特價標示，你知道若是想買 6 件單價皆為 $20 的特價商品，在能取得最高折扣的狀況下，分別得花多少錢嗎？

1	Up to 50% off selected items	$
2	Buy 1 get 1 free	$
3	Buy one get 2nd 50% off	$
4	Buy 2 get 1 free	$
5	Additional 15% off on already reduced prices	$
6	25% off your entire purchase	$
7	15% off clearance items	$
8	Spend $50 save 10%	$
9	Take an extra 50% off all red tag sale items	$
10	$10 off every $50 purchase	$

Ch 8

....

Answer

1	部分精選商品五折起	→ $20×6×50% ＝ $60	$60
2	買一送一	→ $20×3 ＝ $60	$60
3	第二件五折	→ $20×3 ＋ $20×50%×3 ＝ $90	$90
4	買二送一	→ $20×4 ＝ $80	$80
5	特價商品再打八五折	→ $20×6×85% ＝ $102	$102
6	結帳金額再打八折	→ $20×6×75% ＝ $90	$90
7	清倉商品八五折	→ $20×6×85% ＝ $102	$102
8	消費滿五十元打九折	→ $20×6×90% ＝ $108	$108
9	紅標商品全面五折	→ $20×6×50% ＝ $60	$60
10	每消費五十元折十元	→ $20×6 － 20 ＝ $100	$100

Step 3

搞懂了標示，Carrie 開始選購衣物了。不過要找到對的尺寸和喜愛的顏色，有時可得求助店員幫忙了。

Carrie now gets the idea of those sale signs. Time for shopping! However, sometimes it's hard for her to find her size and favorite colors, so she asks the clerks for help.

🔑 Key Expressions

常用的衣物尺寸或顏色詢問句型如下：

Does	clothing	come		in	1. specific size or color
Do you have	clothing				2. unspecific size
Can I get					3. unspecific color

✏️ Exercise 2

請根據中文翻譯，填入相對應的問句。填完後請聽音檔確認答案。（答案在第142頁）

1 Asking for a **specific** size or color: 🎧 Track 16

Carrie: Excuse me. Do you have this shirt (1)＿＿＿＿＿＿？（你們有藍色嗎？）

Salesperson: Yes, we do. Do you want me to get it for you?

- -

Carrie: Excuse me. Does this shirt (2)＿＿＿＿＿？（這有六號嗎？）

Salesperson: Yes, it does. Let me get it for you.

- -

Carrie: Excuse me. Can I get this shirt (3)＿＿＿＿＿？（可以給我小號的嗎？）

Salesperson: Sure. I'll be right back.

2 Asking for an **unspecific** size: 🎧 Track 17

Carrie: Excuse me. Do you have this shirt (4)＿＿＿＿＿？（有小件一點的嗎？）

Salesperson: Sure. Let me see ... it's large. I'll get a medium for you.

3 Asking for an **unspecific** color: 🎧 Track 18

Carrie: Excuse me. Does this shirt (5)＿＿＿＿＿？（有其他顏色嗎？）

Salesperson: Yes, it comes in three other colors, blue, gray and white.

- -

Carrie: Excuse me. Do you have this shirt (6)＿＿＿＿＿？（有其他顏色嗎？）

Salesperson: Yes, we also have blue, gray and white.

Step 4

挑選好了幾件衣物後，接著當然得試穿。雖然部分店家開放讓顧客自行進入更衣間，但也有些店家要求顧客先告知店員，有時甚至會有試穿件數限制。另外，遇到積極的店員，對方可是會主動詢問是否有試穿需求喔。

After picking out some clothes, she'd like to try them on for sure. Although some stores allow customers to freely try clothes on in the fitting rooms, others will ask customers to inform the clerks before they do so, or have a limit on the number of items you can take into the fitting room.

✏ Exercise 3

請聽以下四則 Carrie 和銷售員的對話，並於空格中填入適當的詞語。

- fitting room   ■ name   ■ size   ■ fit   ■ suit

1 In the store (Looking for a fitting room): 🎧 Track 19

Carrie: Hi, where can I try this on?

Salesperson: The fitting rooms are over there.

························ (three minutes later) ························

Salesperson: How does it (1)_____?

Carrie: Pretty good. I'll take it.

2 In the fitting room (Item limits): 🎧 Track 20

Carrie: Hi, I'd like to try these on please.

Salesperson: OK. How many items do you have?

Carrie: Uh ... six.

Salesperson: (Open a room) Here you go. Let me know if you need a different (2)_____.

························ (ten minutes later) ························

Salesperson: Any good?

Carrie: No, not really. They don't really (3)_____ me well.

3 In the store (Aggressive approach): 🎧 Track 21

Salesperson: Hi, are you finding everything OK? Would you like to try this on?

Carrie: Yes, please.

Salesperson: Alright. I'll put it in the (4)_____ for you.

--- (three minutes later) ---

Salesperson: You look cute on that skirt.

Carrie: Thanks.

4 In the store (Aggressive approach): 🎧 Track 22

Salesperson: Hi, can I set up a room for you?

Carrie: Yes, that would be great.

Salesperson: Your (5) _____, please?

Carrie: Carrie.

Salesperson: No problem.

Answer Exercise 2

(1) in blue   (2) come in size 6   (3) in a small   (4) in a smaller size

(5) come in any other colors   (6) in any other colors

Answer Exercise 3

(1) fit   (2) size   (3) suit   (4) fitting room   (5) name

💡 **try on** 試穿。此片語可拆，要試穿的衣物可置於其中或其後。

例如：try this shirt on = try on this shirt

💡 **fitting room = dressing room = changing room** 更衣間

💡 **You look cute on that skirt.** 這裡用 on 類似「穿上」put on 的用法，可以想成把人放在衣物上，後接衣物。該句也可將人和衣物的位置倒過來說，例如：The skirt looks good on you. 變成衣物放在人身上。

💡 **fit vs. suit** 用 fit 多指尺寸上的適合，而 suit 則是指風格如顏色、樣式上的適合。

例如：
It fits me very well.（正是我的尺寸。）
It suits me very well.（我穿起來很好看。）

Word	Meaning
selected (*a.*)	chosen in preference to another or others 經過挑選的
item (*n.*)	an individual thing; a separate part or thing 項目；品項
additional (*a.*)	more than is usual or expected 額外的；附加的
reduced (*a.*)	made smaller in size, amount, number, etc. 減少的；降低的
entire (*a.*)	having all the parts or elements; whole; complete 全部的；完全的
clearance sale (*n.*)	a sale to clear out stock 清倉拍賣
extra (*a.*)	more than what is usual or necessary; additional 額外的
tag (*n.*)	a piece or strip of paper, leather, etc., as a mark or label 標籤
purchase (*n.*)	something that is obtained by paying money 購買品
specific (*a.*)	clearly and exactly presented or stated 特殊的；明確的
limit (*n.*)	an amount or number that is the highest or lowest allowed 限制；限度
aggressive (*a.*)	positive and forceful with energy 積極的

終於試穿完畢想買的衣物，Carrie 準備到櫃台結帳了。不過 Carrie 可以選擇哪些付款方式呢？而櫃台邊的退貨規定又該注意什麼呢？

✎ Exercise 1

購買衣物時，店內付款方式有以下幾種，你還記得它們的英文嗎？

1 by 信用卡 _____
2 by 現金卡 _____
3 in 現金 _____
4 by 支票 _____ （非每間店都收）
5 by 旅行支票 _____ （非每間店都收）

✎ Exercise 2

除了櫃台旁，一般店家的收據上也多會印上退換貨規定。請閱讀以下退換貨規定。
（翻譯在第229頁）

Lady House Return Policy

If you are not satisfied with your purchase, you may return or exchange it within 30 days of the purchase date. The merchandise must be unworn, unwashed, or unaltered in any way and must have all tags attached. Returns are available of any of our Lady House stores nationwide.

Original sales receipt must accompany merchandise to issue a return or exchange. Refunds will be issued in the original form of payment only. Refund checks are subject to a service charge of $25.

Returns made after 30 days of the purchase date and any final sale merchandise are not subject to refund or exchange.

※ 本頁練習的答案在第 147 頁。

根據前一頁的退換貨規定，請試著回答下列資訊。

Acceptable return or exchange period: (1) _____

Acceptable return condition: (2) _____

Return locations: (3) _____

Proof of purchase: (4) _____

The fee for a refund check: (5) _____

🔑 Key Words

Word	Meaning
merchandise (*n.*)	goods that are bought and sold 商品；貨物
unworn (*a.*)	not worn 未受損的
unaltered (*a.*)	not changed or modified 未被改變或修改過的
attached (*a.*)	joined or connected to something 附加的；附屬的
nationwide (*a.*)	throughout a whole nation 全國的
receipt (*n.*)	a piece of paper listing things purchased and the prices paid 收據
accompany (*v.*)	to go together with something; to be included with something 伴隨
issue (*v.*)	to distribute officially 核發；發給
refund (*n.*)	an amount of money that is given back to someone who has returned a product 退款

請聽 Carrie 和銷售員的對話，並於空格中填入適當的詞語。

- $250.47   ■ 30   ■ checks   ■ traveler's checks   ■ credit card
- on sale   ■ return policy   ■ returns   ■ cash   ■ receipt

Salesperson:	Hi, will that be all for you? Do you want anything else?
Carrie:	No, thanks. That's it.
Salesperson:	Was anyone helping you today?
Carrie:	Yes. I think her name is Katherine.
Salesperson:	OK.
Carrie:	Oh ... can you check the price of this for me? Is it (1)_____?
Salesperson:	Let me see ... yes, it's on sale with a discount of (2)_____ percent.
Carrie:	Great, thanks.
Salesperson:	So your total comes to (3)_____. Will that be cash or charge?
Carrie:	Do you accept (4)_____?
Salesperson:	No, I'm sorry. We don't accept any kinds of (5)_____.
Carrie:	That's fine. I'll just pay by (6)_____. Oh ... no! I left my card at home. Alright, guess I can only pay in (7)_____.
Salesperson:	Here is your change. Do you want your (8)_____ in the bag or with you?
Carrie:	In the bag please. By the way, do you accept (9)_____?
Salesperson:	Yes, we do. Our (10)_____ is printed on the receipt below the product description.
Carrie:	Thank you.
Salesperson:	You're welcome and have a nice day.

Key Words

Word	Meaning
discount (*n.*)	an amount taken off a regular price 折扣
come to (*v. phr.*)	amount to a sum of money 總計
description (*n.*)	a statement that tells you how something or someone looks, sounds, etc. 描述；形容

146

Answer Exercise 1

1 credit card   2 debit card   3 cash   4 check   5 traveler's check

Answer Exercise 2

(1) within 30 days of the purchase date

(2) items that are unworn, unwashed, or unaltered in any way and must have all tags attached

(3) any Lady House store nationwide

(4) original sales receipt

(5) $25

Answer Exercise 3

(1) on sale   (2) 30   (3) $250.47   (4) traveler's checks   (5) checks

(6) credit card   (7) cash   (8) receipt   (9) returns   (10) return policy

Ch 8

Task 1 Crossword Puzzle 填字遊戲

請根據下列英文提示，將該單字填入空格中。Hint: 可參考前面的 Key Words 表。

Across:

2. made smaller in size, amount, number, etc.

5. chosen in preference to another or others

6. an amount or number that is the highest or lowest allowed

7. a piece or strip of paper, as a mark or label

9. something that is obtained by paying money

Down:

1. a separate part or thing

3. more than what is usual or necessary; additional

4. having all the parts or elements; whole

8. clearly and exactly presented or stated

10. positive and forceful with energy

Task 2 Matching 配對

請於左列的英文字中，找出和右方的中文字義相對應者。

1 merchandise	_____	
2 unworn	_____	
3 unaltered	_____	
4 attached	_____	
5 nationwide	_____	
6 receipt	_____	
7 accompany	_____	
8 issue	_____	
9 refund	_____	
10 discount	_____	

A	附屬的
B	伴隨
C	收據
D	未受損的
E	核發
F	商品
G	退款
H	折扣
I	全國的
J	未被改變或修改過的

Ch 8

CHAPTER SUMMARY

Get to know the basic elements of an advertisement.
了解特價廣告上的資訊元素。

- **item** 品項
- **original price** 原價
- **sale price / discounted price** 特價
- **discount percentage** 折數
- **sale time** 折扣期
- **store name** 店名

Recognize the various sale signs in a store.
辨識店內各種特價標示。

★ 中英文標示折數的方式不同，中文打 2 折，英文是 80% off 喔！

Ask for different sizes or colors, and try the clothes on in a fitting room.
詢問尺寸和顏色，在更衣間試穿。

Choose the payment options.
選擇付款方式。

- **by credit card** 信用卡
- **by check** 支票
- **by debit card** 金融卡
- **by traveler's check** 旅行支票
- **in cash** 現金

Read the terms of the return policy.
閱讀退換貨規定條款。

Q 請根據這篇文章，回答下列問題。

Return Policy
No Refunds
Exchanges Only

Items returned in original condition may be exchanged for other merchandise or store credit within 45 days of your purchase and must be accompanied by the original receipt.

Please visit our website at www.happyshopping.com for more information on our return policy. Also, our service representatives would be happy to answer your questions over the phone.

Contact number: 810-337-5911

What items are required to exchange the merchandise?

(A) The product and the sales receipt

(B) The product and the credit card

(C) The sales receipt and the credit card

(D) Extra cash and the original packaging

Answer A

Chapter 9

Mail Services
郵件服務

在本章，你將會學習到如何寄送郵件和包裹。

Situation: Mail Packages 寄包裹

終於安頓好了，不過 Carrie 卻想起下週就是自己好友的生日。雖然人在國外無法幫好友慶生，可總得寄個禮物祝賀一下。然而禮物挑好了，到了郵局，Carrie 卻不知道該怎麼寄出。

☆ 你能陪她一塊完成包裹寄送嗎？

Work Schedule

⊘ Calculate International Postage 計算國際郵資
⊘ Get to Know More about International Mailing Services
　　了解更多有關國際郵件服務

Flat-rate Service 均一價服務

到郵局寄信或包裹有許多選擇，主要依預計的送達時間而有所不同。當然，想愈快寄達，索費也會愈高。另外，距離遠近和重量大小，也都是影響價格的因素。不想被郵資嚇到，就得先搞清楚最有利於自己的寄件方式。

Step 1

想知道美國郵局有提供哪些寄件選擇，連上其網站就可以查詢到。快上去看看吧！

Get on the US Postal Service website and you can easily find out the shipping services the USPS offers. Try it yourself now!

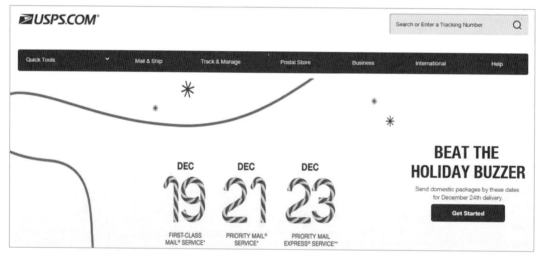

<Website> https://www.usps.com/

Step 2

想寄國際包裹的 Carrie 點選了 International 之後，發現左邊居然還有一堆欄位可選，到底各個欄位有什麼作用呢？

Carrie finds that there are still a lot of menu items to choose from after she clicks "International" on the top-right. What does each column mean?

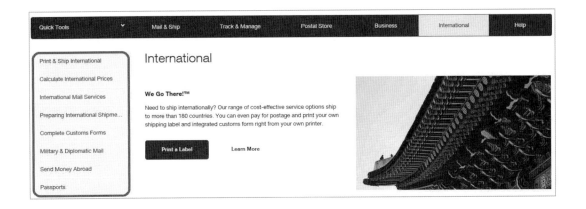

✏️ Exercise 1

網頁左欄有許多選單如下，利用你看懂的詞彙猜猜看它們各代表什麼意思吧！

_____ **1** Print & Ship International	
_____ **2** Calculate International Prices	
_____ **3** International Mail Services	
_____ **4** Preparing International Shipment	
_____ **5** Complete Customs Forms	
_____ **6** Military & Diplomatic Mail	
_____ **7** Send Money Abroad	
_____ **8** Passports	

a	準備國際運送，包含了解尺寸大小規定、禁寄物品、封面書寫方式、打包方式等
b	寄送申辦新護照或更新護照之文件
c	列印運送資料的標籤
d	填寫海關申報單
e	寄送給軍人或外交人員
f	計算國際寄件費用
g	國際寄件服務選擇
h	寄送郵局匯票到國外

Step 3

從未在美國寄過件的 Carrie 最想知道的當然是價格，點選第 2 項後發現要填的資料不少，有些什麼呢？快進去看看吧！

Carrie has never sent a package internationally. Surely, she's more interested in the prices. However, she finds a lot of boxes to fill in on the webpage. What are they?

....

Answer

1 c　　　2 f　　　3 g　　　4 a　　　5 d　　　6 e　　　7 h　　　8 b

Ch 9

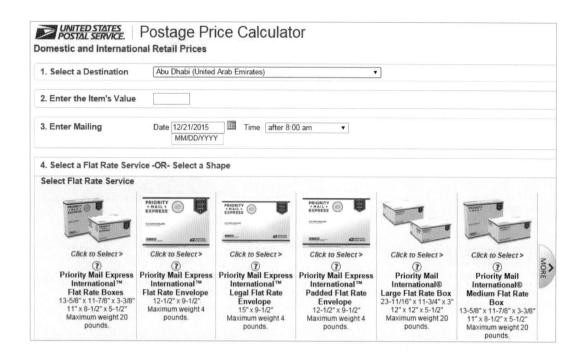

UNITED STATES POSTAL SERVICE. | Postage Price Calculator

Domestic and International Retail Prices

1. Select a Destination — Abu Dhabi (United Arab Emirates) ▼

2. Enter the Item's Value — [ ]

3. Enter Mailing — Date 12/21/2015   Time after 8:00 am ▼
MM/DD/YYYY

4. Select a Flat Rate Service -OR- Select a Shape

Select Flat Rate Service

Click to Select >	Click to Select >	Click to Select >	Click to Select >	Click to Select >	Click to Select >
Priority Mail Express International™ Flat Rate Boxes 13-5/8" x 11-7/8" x 3-3/8" 11" x 8-1/2" x 5-1/2" Maximum weight 20 pounds.	Priority Mail Express International™ Flat Rate Envelope 12-1/2" x 9-1/2" Maximum weight 4 pounds.	Priority Mail Express International™ Legal Flat Rate Envelope 15" x 9-1/2" Maximum weight 4 pounds.	Priority Mail Express International™ Padded Flat Rate Envelope 12-1/2" x 9-1/2" Maximum weight 4 pounds.	Priority Mail International® Large Flat Rate Box 23-11/16" x 11-3/4" x 3" 12" x 12" x 5-1/2" Maximum weight 20 pounds.	Priority Mail International® Medium Flat Rate Box 13-5/8" x 11-7/8" x 3-3/8" 11" x 8-1/2" x 5-1/2" Maximum weight 20 pounds.

MORE

 **Exercise 2**   Track 24

請聽 Carrie 和 Steven 的對話，並於空格中填入適當的詞語。

- select
- webisite
- weight
- value
- postal service
- flat rate

Carrie: Thank God. You're home!

Steven: What's going on, Carrie?

Carrie: Oh, I'm planning to mail a gift back to Taiwan. But you know ... I've never used the international (1)_____ before, so I would prefer to know the price beforehand.

Steven: You surely need to. International mail is usually pretty expensive. Do you need the (2)_____? I can find it for you.

Carrie: Actually, I'm stuck on that page now.

Steven: How come? Don't you just fill in the boxes?

Carrie: The problem is I don't know what each box is asking for. Can you come and help me with that?

Steven: OK, let me see ... Select a destination. For this, you simply select the place you would like to send your gift to. Taiwan, isn't it?

Carrie: Right.

Steven: Then enter the (3)_____ of your gift.

Carrie: The gift? It's $120. And the mailing date here is today, isn't it?

Steven: Bingo!

Carrie: Alright. Guess the next step is to (4)_____ the right "mail shape" for my gift, but what does (5)_____ mean?

Steven: It means they <u>charge</u> you a <u>fixed</u> price for the same size of envelope or package, regardless of the (6)_____, as long as the item can be fit in. Wait, I missed this .... For each option, they do have a <u>maximum</u> weight. So make sure your gift doesn't <u>exceed</u> that.

Carrie: Got it. Thanks.

Answer

(1) postal service   (2) website   (3) value   (4) select   (5) flat rate

(6) weight

🗝 **Thank God. = Thank goodness. = Thank heaven.** 表示「謝天謝地」的感嘆句。

🗝 **What's going on? = What's happing? = What's wrong?** 是詢問對方「發生什麼事了」好用句，不論大小事都可以使用喔！

🗝 **prefer to (V)** 「較喜歡做某事」的意思。另外，若是拆開來 prefer A to B 則意味「喜歡 A 勝於 B」。

🗝 **How come ...** 「怎麼會……？」的意思，和 why 差不多。

🗝 **ask for (something)** ask 本意可指「詢問」，但還可作「請求」解，這裡 ask for 就是「要求某物」之意。

🗝 **Bingo!** 此字由來為「賓果遊戲」，遊戲最後大家都會喊 Bingo! 表示已完成任務，因此平常使用時，可指他人剛才所言正確，即「你說對了」之意。

🗝 **regardless of; in spite of; despite** 不管

🗝 **as long as** 「只要」，作連接詞使用。至於 as far as 則是「達到……的程度」；「盡……」。

🔑 **Key Words**

Word	Meaning
calculate (*v.*)	to find the number or amount of something by mathematical means 計算
shipment (*n.*)	the act of sending goods 運送
complete (*v.*)	to finish doing something 完成
customs (*n.*)	the taxes you pay on goods that you bring from one country to another 關稅
form (*n.*)	a printed document with blank spaces to fill in information 表單
beforehand (*adv.*)	before an action or event 事先；預先
stuck (*a.*)	unable to change a situation 困住；卡住
destination (*n.*)	the place where someone is going or something is being sent 目的地
charge (*v.*)	to ask payment 索費
fixed (*a.*)	not changing 不變的
maximum (*n.*)	the largest in amount, size, or number allowed 最大值
exceed (*v.*)	to go above the limit 超過

Step 4

雖了解了各項資訊，可最後的郵件包裝卻因有太多選擇，讓 Carrie 搞不清楚該選哪個好，看一看，到底有哪些種類呢？

Finally Carrie figures out what to fill in for each box. However, for the flat rate service, there are many options. Let's see what they are.

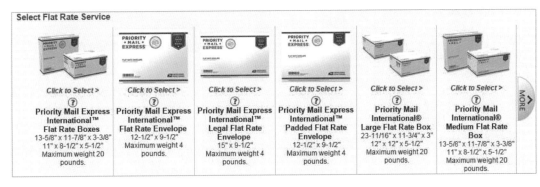

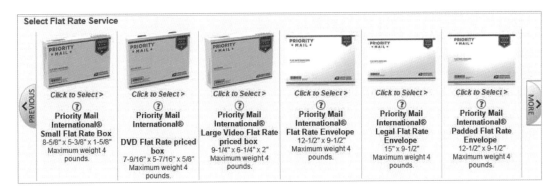

✏️ Exercise 3

原來郵件包裝主要分爲信封和盒子，不過還有其他的差異。請根據上圖，將資訊填入表格內吧！

Options 郵寄方式	Express 特快	Size 尺寸	Max. Weight (pounds) 重量上限	Contents 內容物	Padded 氣泡袋
Priority Mail Express International Flat Rate Boxes					
Priority Mail Express International Flat Rate Envelope					
Priority Mail Express International Legal Flat Rate Envelope	✓	■ 15" × 9-1/2"	4	Legal documents	
Priority Mail Express International Padded Flat Rate Envelope	✓	■ 12-1/2" × 9-1/2"	4		✓
Priority Mail International Large Flat Rate Box					
Priority Mail International Medium Flat Rate Box					
Priority Mail International Small Flat Rate Box					
Priority Mail International DVD Flat Rate Priced Box					
Priority Mail International Large Video Flat Rate Priced Box					
Priority Mail International Flat Rate Envelope					

Options 郵寄方式	Express 特快	Size 尺寸	Max. Weight (pounds) 重量上限	Contents 內容物	Padded 氣泡袋
Priority Mail International Legal Flat Rate Envelope					
Priority Mail International Padded Flat Rate Envelope					

Key Words

Word	Meaning
express (*n.*)	a rapid delivery service 快遞
content (*n.*)	the things that are included 內容物
padded (*a.*)	filling or stuffing with a soft material 有裝填墊料的
legal (*a.*)	relating to the law 法律上的

Answer

Options	Express	Size	Max. Weight	Contents	Padded
Priority Mail Express International Flat Rate Boxes	✓	■ 13-5/8" × 11-7/8" × 3-3/8" ■ 11" × 8-1/2" × 5-1/2"	20		
Priority Mail Express International Flat Rate Envelope	✓	■ 12-1/2" × 9-1/2"	4		
Priority Mail Express International Legal Flat Rate Envelope	✓	■ 15" × 9-1/2"	4	Legal documents	
Priority Mail Express International Padded Flat Rate Envelope	✓	■ 12-1/2" × 9-1/2"	4		✓
Priority Mail International Large Flat Rate Box		■ 23-11/16" × 11-3/4" × 3" ■ 12" × 12" × 5-1/2"	20		
Priority Mail International Medium Flat Rate Box		■ 13-5/8" × 11-7/8" × 3-3/8" ■ 11" × 8-1/2" × 5-1/2"	20		

Ch
9

Options	Express	Size	Max. Weight	Contents	Padded
Priority Mail International Small Flat Rate Box		■ 8-5/8" × 5-3/8" × 1-5/8"	4		
Priority Mail International DVD Flat Rate Priced Box		■ 7-9/16" × 5-7/16" × 5/8"	4	DVD	
Priority Mail International Large Video Flat Rate Priced Box		■ 9-1/4" × 6-1/4" × 2"	4	Video	
Priority Mail International Flat Rate Envelope		■ 12-1/2" × 9-1/2"	4		
Priority Mail International Legal Flat Rate Envelope		■ 15" × 9-1/2"	4	Legal documents	
Priority Mail International Padded Flat Rate Envelope		■ 12-1/2" × 9-1/2"	4		✓

註 11" × 8-1/2" × 5-1/2" 意思為 11 吋 (inch) × 8.5 吋 × 5.5 吋。

Exercise 4

填完上表之後，可以了解各種包裝的大致差異。請根據以下敘述，幫幫 Carrie 找到合適的郵件包裝吧！

★ 禮物是一只約 1 磅重的手錶，Carrie 很怕被摔壞，她希望可以愈快寄到愈好。

Answer

Priority Mail Express International Padded Flat Rate Envelope

TASK 2 Get to Know More about International Mailing Services

Speed of Delivery 郵遞速度

雖然知道 Express 是表示快速送達，但到底可以多快？時間上的選擇有哪些呢？從首頁進入「國際郵件服務」瞧瞧吧！

<Website> https://www.usps.com/international/mail-shipping-services.htm

✏️ **Exercise 1**

進入網頁後，試著將下列缺少的資訊補上吧！（翻譯在第231頁）

Global Express Guaranteed®

(1) _____ Business Days

Global Express Guaranteed® (GXG®) service provides our fastest international shipping services. Get competitive international shipping rates and (2) _____ international delivery with a (3) _____ to more than 180 countries. International transportation and delivery provided by FedEx Express. From $(4) _____.

Priority Mail Express International®

(5) _____ Business Days

Affordable and fast international delivery to more than 180 countries with a money-back guarantee to select countries. (6) _____ international shipping prices and free shipping supplies available. Discounts off retail prices may be available when purchasing online. From $(7) _____.

Ch 9

Priority Mail International®

(8) _____ Business Days

Reliable and affordable way to send mail and packages to more than 180 countries.
Plus, get Flat Rate international shipping pricing, free shipping supplies, and

(9) _____ off retail prices may be available when purchasing online. From

$(10) _____ .

✎ Exercise 2

但除了上述選擇外，若不在意送達時間稍晚，並能自己提供包裝的材料，其實還
有其他兩種選擇，找找同一網頁資訊幫忙將空格補上吧！（翻譯在第231頁）

First-Class Mail International®

Affordable International Service

Our most affordable option for (1) _____ , (2) _____ , and

(3) _____ . Send anything up to (4) _____ lbs (cannot exceed

$(5) _____ in value) to more than 180 countries. From $(6) _____ at
a Post Office.

First-Class Package International Service®

Affordable International Service

An economical way to send small packages to more than 180 countries. Send anything
up to 4 lbs (cannot exceed $400 in value). From $(7) _____ .

....

Answer Exercise 1

(1) 1-3	(2) date-certain	(3) money-back guarantee	(4) 55.85	(5) 3-5
(6) Flat Rate	(7) 38.00	(8) 6-10	(9) discounts	(10) 37.50

Answer Exercise 2

(1) postcards	(2) envelopes	(3) flats	(4) 4	(5) 400
(6) 1.20	(7) 7.10			

✎ Exercise 3

Carrie 總算搞懂了寄件的選擇，可為了預防自己寄到不該寄的，還是先確認一下禁寄品有哪些比較好。你知道這些禁寄品為何嗎？連連看吧。（答案在第167頁）

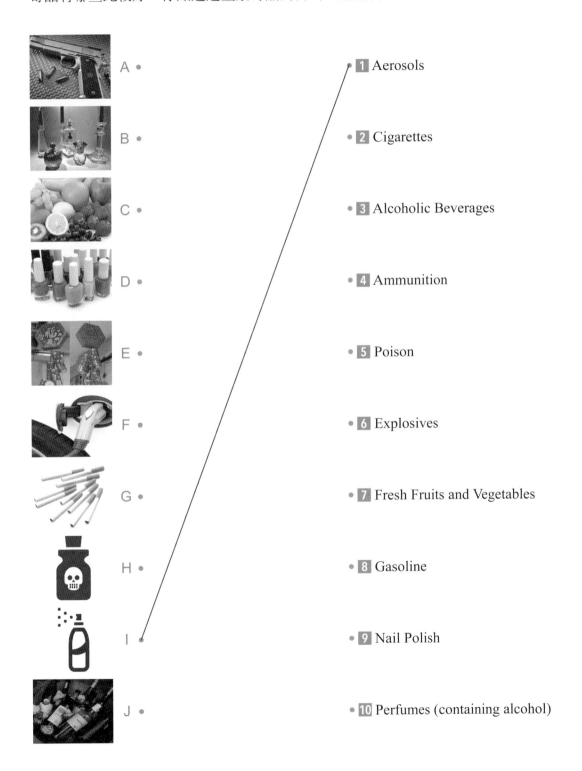

A •

B •

C •

D •

E •

F •

G •

H •

I •

J •

1 Aerosols

2 Cigarettes

3 Alcoholic Beverages

4 Ammunition

5 Poison

6 Explosives

7 Fresh Fruits and Vegetables

8 Gasoline

9 Nail Polish

10 Perfumes (containing alcohol)

Ch
9

Exercise 4

目前為止一切順利，接著最後就是要填寫海關的報關單了。你知道下面各標題代表甚麼意思嗎？

PS Form **2976-A,** May 2009 PSN: 7530-01-000-9834

1	2	3
4	5	6
7	8	9
10	11	12
13	14	15
16	17	

18 （由上而下，由左至右）禮物、文件、商品、退貨、樣品、其他

19 空運、海運　　　20 _____　　21 _____

22 丟棄、退回給寄件者、改寄到下列地址　　23 _____

166

1 噴霧劑 = I 2 菸 = G 3 酒精飲料 = J 4 彈藥 = A 5 毒藥 = H

6 爆裂物 = E 7 新鮮蔬果 = C 8 汽油 = F 9 指甲油 = D 10 香水 = B

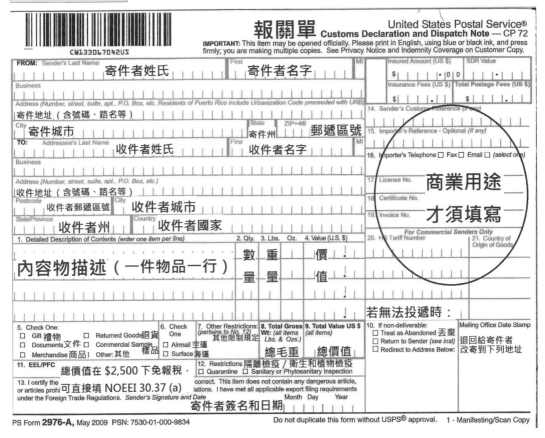

<Website> http://about.usps.com/forms/ps2976a.pdf

Task 1 Crossword Puzzle 填字遊戲

請根據下列英文提示，將該單字填入空格中。Hint: 可參考前面的 Key Words 表。

Across:

1. the taxes you pay on goods that you bring from one country to another

3. the things that are included

5. the place where someone is going or something is being sent

6. a rapid delivery service

8. to finish doing something

168

9. to find the number or amount of something by mathematical means

11. relating to the law

13. a printed document with blank spaces to fill in information

14. to go above the limit

15. the largest in amount, size, or number allowed

Down:

2. the act of sending goods

4. not changing

7. filling or stuffing with a soft material

9. to ask for payment

10. before an action or event

12. unable to change a situation

Answer

1. customs	2. shipment	3. content	4. fixed
5. destination	6. express	7. padded	8. complete
9. calculate (ACROSS)	9. charge (DOWN)	10. beforehand	11. legal
12. stuck	13. form	14. exceed	15. maximum

Task 2 Word Search 找字

請於下表中找出以下這些詞彙。Hint: 答案有可能是右到左或下到上排列。

■ AFFORDABLE   ■ CERTAIN   ■ DELIVERY   ■ ECONOMICAL
■ GUARANTEED   ■ PROVIDE   ■ RETAIL   ■ SUPPLY

Y	R	X	Z	T	O	J	E	G	U	U	H	X	M	J
A	R	E	N	H	Y	N	D	U	K	C	K	L	W	K
Y	O	E	T	D	I	S	I	A	S	U	P	P	L	Y
S	O	S	V	A	P	O	V	R	Z	X	V	N	Y	N
W	D	J	T	I	I	R	O	A	C	P	V	X	A	T
T	G	R	L	Z	L	L	R	N	U	D	V	F	Y	T
Z	E	S	N	Q	U	E	P	T	Z	W	F	K	D	A
C	Q	U	G	I	C	L	D	E	H	O	J	T	O	D
O	Z	J	G	U	F	J	Q	E	R	T	A	E	P	X
V	I	Z	O	L	R	J	G	D	I	Q	A	C	Q	D
I	Y	Y	F	P	D	U	A	Q	Q	C	V	Z	F	S
E	S	G	H	Q	R	B	L	Q	V	U	K	G	X	A
L	B	A	P	G	L	A	C	I	M	O	N	O	C	E
C	R	M	K	E	T	Q	X	G	Z	X	P	D	X	W
T	Q	P	A	P	M	J	O	B	B	S	L	V	X	H

170

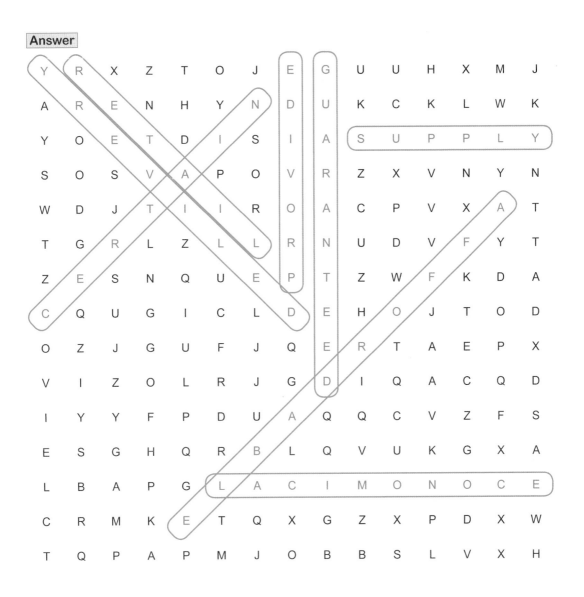

Y	R	X	Z	T	O	J	E	G	U	U	H	X	M	J
A	R	E	N	H	Y	N	D	U	K	C	K	L	W	K
Y	O	E	T	D	I	S	I	A	S	U	P	P	L	Y
S	O	S	V	A	P	O	V	R	Z	X	V	N	Y	N
W	D	J	T	I	I	R	O	A	C	P	V	X	A	T
T	G	R	L	Z	L	L	R	N	U	D	V	F	Y	T
Z	E	S	N	Q	U	E	P	T	Z	W	F	K	D	A
C	Q	U	G	I	C	L	D	E	H	O	J	T	O	D
O	Z	J	G	U	F	J	Q	E	R	T	A	E	P	X
V	I	Z	O	L	R	J	G	D	I	Q	A	C	Q	D
I	Y	Y	F	P	D	U	A	Q	Q	C	V	Z	F	S
E	S	G	H	Q	R	B	L	Q	V	U	K	G	X	A
L	B	A	P	G	L	A	C	I	M	O	N	O	C	E
C	R	M	K	E	T	Q	X	G	Z	X	P	D	X	W
T	Q	P	A	P	M	J	O	B	B	S	L	V	X	H

CHAPTER SUMMARY

Get on the USPS website and then select "International."
搜尋美國郵局網站後選擇國際郵件服務。

↓

Calculate the postage. 計算郵資。

 必填資料有：

• **Destination** 目的地　　• **Item's Value** 物品價值　　• **Mailing Date** 寄送日
• **Flat Rate Service** 包裝選擇（均一價）

↓

Get to know more about international mailing services.
了解更多有關國際郵件服務。

★不知哪種適合的話，可在網頁上點選 "Quick Compare" 看比較。

 按寄送時間長短主要有：

• **Global Express Guaranteed (1-3 Business Days)**
• **Priority Mail Express International (3-5 Business Days)**
• **Priority Mail International (6-10 Business Days)**

↓

Check the restricted & prohibited items. 查看有哪些禁寄品。

 易錯寄物品有：

• **Aerosols** 噴霧劑　　　• **Cigarettes** 香菸　　　• **Perfumes** 香水
• **Fresh fruits and vegetables** 新鮮蔬果　　• **Nail polish** 指甲油

↓

Complete the customs form. 填寫海關的報關單。

Q 請聽音檔播放的問題與選項，並從中選出最適合的回應。

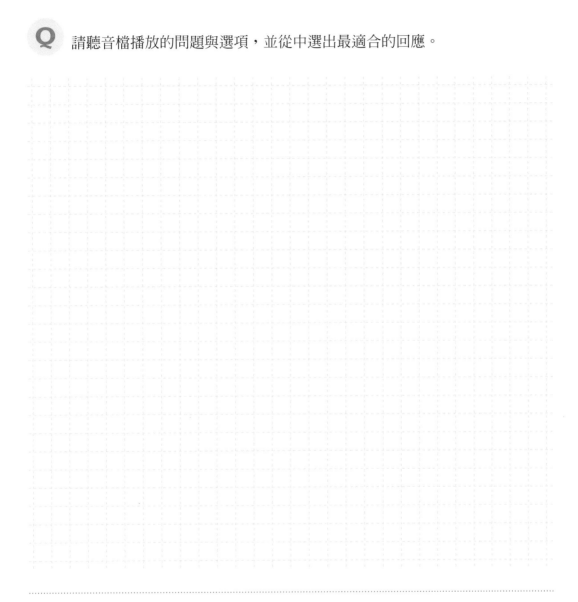

Ch
9

Script

Hi, I'd like to mail this package to Taiwan, please.

A. Whose letter is it?

B. It's packaged in a small box.

C. How would you like to send it?

Answer C

Chapter 10

Choosing a Phone Plan
選擇手機方案

在本章，你將會學習到如何選擇適合自己的通話方案。

Situation: Make a Phone Call 打電話

寄送了禮物，擔心好友錯過收件時間，Carrie 想想還是打個電話提醒一下對方好了。可拿起手機這才發現，她還沒有申請美國電話呢！ Carrie 趕緊前往附近的電信公司詢問。

☆ 你能陪她一塊完成方案挑選嗎？

Work Schedule

⊘ Get to Know Each Plan 了解方案

⊘ Other Plan Options 其他選擇

TASK 1　Get to Know Each Plan

Prepaid Plans 預付卡方案

美國較為普及的電信公司有 T-Mobile、AT&T、Verizon 和 Sprint 這幾家。各家推出的優惠方案不同，可以先上網查詢。不過除了方案外，大多數人在選擇電信公司時，其實也很常考量以其所在位置的收訊強弱來決定。

Step 1

要知道有什麼通話方案可以選擇，當然得連上它們的網站瞧瞧。試試 T-Mobile，連上後該從哪個選項進行下一步呢？

Let's get on some cell phone carriers' websites and see what plans they offer. Below is the homepage of T-Mobile. So what should we click next?

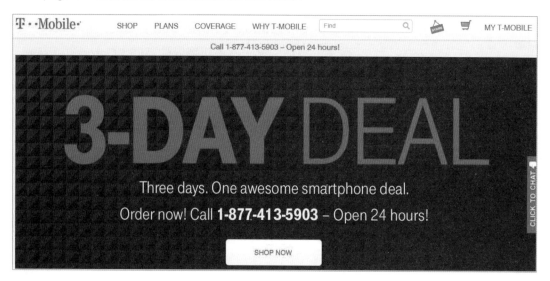

<Website> http://www.t-mobile.com/

其他電信業者網站：

AT&T　(http://www.att.com/)

Verizon　(http://www.verizonwireless.com/)

Sprint　(https://www.sprint.com/)

Answer

PLANS

Step 2

從「方案」選單點入後，竟又再細分成三項，各有那些特點呢？點進去各方案網頁後試著歸類吧！

Click "PLANS" and we see that there are three options. Look at each plan and categorize its features!

Plans	Credit check	Calls and texts	Internet	Suitable for individual	Suitable for family
Voice plans	✓				
Mobile Internet plans	✓				
Prepaid plans					

Answer

Plans 方案	Credit check 信用審核	Calls and texts 打電話和收發簡訊	Internet 網路	Suitable for individual 適合個人	Suitable for family 適合家庭
Voice plans 通話	✓	✓	✓		✓
Mobile Internet plans 行動上網	✓		✓	✓	
Prepaid plans 預付卡		✓	✓	✓	✓

Ch
10

註 除了 prepaid plans（預付卡），其他方案一般都是月費制，在國外基本上都需要做信用審核 (credit check)，尤其是若顧客想分期購買新機，須參與 Equipment Installment Plan (EIP) 時。

Step 3

Carrie 才剛到美國，沒有信用紀錄，看來只能先辦預付卡了。網頁出現三種通話方案，Carrie 該選哪個呢？

Clearly, Carries can't run a credit check as she's new in the States. Guess prepaid plans will be the best choice for her. Look at the three different voice plans under prepaid plans, which one should Carrie select?

Affordable voice plans

Whether you need a plan for yourself or for your family, our prepaid voice plans have you covered.

Individual plans

We doubled the 4G LTE data on our Simple Choice plan – at the same price.

See Simple Choice plans ➤

Family plans

Now for a limited time, families can get 4 lines, each with 6 GB of 4G LTE data for $30 per line.

See family plans ➤

Family plans are postpaid; deposit may be req'd.

Pay as you go

Plan starts at just $3/mo.

See pay as you go plans ➤

<Website> http://prepaid-phones.t-mobile.com/prepaid-plans

....

Answer

Individual plans（個人方案）

Step 4

選擇方案時，你覺得重要的條件有哪些呢？（答案因人而異）

When you choose a plan, what are the key factors to consider?

☐ Price per month 月費

☐ Number of lines 共用方案門號數

☐ Number of texts 簡訊數

☐ Number of minutes 分鐘數

☐ Contract period 合約期

☐ Amount of total data 上網量

☐ Other: _____

點選 Individual plans 底下的 Simple Choice plans，看看圈選的方案內容，試著在下列空格中填入缺少的資訊。

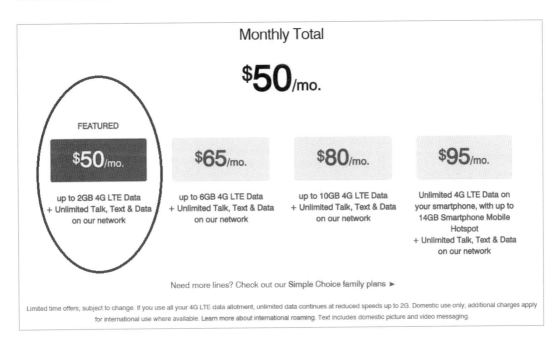

<Website> http://prepaid-phones.t-mobile.com/simple-choice-prepaid-plans

1 Price per month: $ _____

2 Number of lines: _____

3 Number of texts: _____

4 Number of minutes: _____

5 Contract period: _____

6 Amount of total data: _____

✎ **Exercise 2**   🎧 **Track 26**

請聽 Carrie 和客服人員的對話，並於空格中填入適當的詞語。

■ annual   ■ SIM card   ■ overage fees   ■ $50 prepaid monthly plan
■ device's compatibility   ■ BRING YOUR OWN DEVICE

Operator: Hi, T-Mobile. How may I help you?

Carrie: Hi. I'd like to sign up for a phone plan for my cell phone.

Operator: No problem. What plan would you like to get?

Carrie: Actually, I've checked your website, and am very interested in your
(1) _____. But I'm not sure if I need to sign a contract.

Operator: All the phone plans in T-Mobile have no (2) _____ service contracts any more.

Carrie: Sweet! And what about the overage fees? I read that I can use up to 2GB of 4G LTE data. How much do I need to pay if I go over that limit?

Operator: No domestic (3) _____ will be charged. That means if you go over your allocated amount of data, you can still use it, but at a reduced data speed. So besides associated taxes and surcharges, $50 will be all you have to pay.

Carrie: Terrific! I think I'll just get this plan. How do I apply for it?

Operator: Would you like to buy a new phone or use your own device?

Carrie: I don't need a new phone. I have my iPhone with me.

Operator: Well, in that case it's simple. Just get on our T-Mobile website, and click "(4) _____" under "SHOP". Now you'll see three steps. First, you can check your (5) _____. If there's no problem, go to step 2 and be ready to purchase your (6) _____.

🔑 Key Expressions

- **How may I help you? = May I help you?**
  = How can I help you? = What can I do for you?
  是很常見店員或客服人員的開頭語，表示「有什麼我可以服務的」。
- **sign up** 「報名登記」或「簽約」，表示加入某活動或課程。
  例如報名課程就可以說：sign up for the class。
- **Sweet! = Nice! = Terrific!** 表示某事物「很棒、令人滿意」的語氣詞。
- **What about** 用於徵詢對方意見，也可用於提出建議時 = How about。
  注意，about 是介系詞，因此後面須接名詞或動名詞喔！
- **up to** up 本身就有「往上」之意，在此則是表「多達；直到」，後面常接數量。
- **in that case** case 本指「事例」，在此的涵義則類似「在那樣的例子下」，譯為「若是那樣的話」。

🔑 Key Words

Word	Meaning
overage (*n.*)	a supply of goods or services that exceeds a preset limit 超額商品
domestic (*a.*)	within one's own country 國內的
allocate (*v.*)	to set apart and give out to particular people 分派；分配
amount (*n.*)	the total number or quantity 總數；數量
reduced (*a.*)	to make smaller in size, number or degree 減少了的；降低的
speed (*n.*)	the rate that something moves 速率；速度
associated (*a.*)	connected or related to a particular subject, activity etc. 相關的
surcharge (*n.*)	an additional amount of money added to the usual price 額外費；附加費
device (*n.*)	a machine or equipment invented for a particular job 設備；裝置

除了前面介紹的方案，還有沒有更便宜的預付卡方案適合 Carrie ？

✎ Exercise 1

網頁拉到最下面，居然還有更多便宜的選擇，先瞧瞧 Just the basics 為何能比 $50 monthly plan 還便宜？主要差異是什麼？

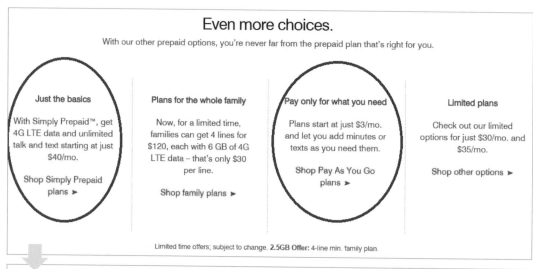

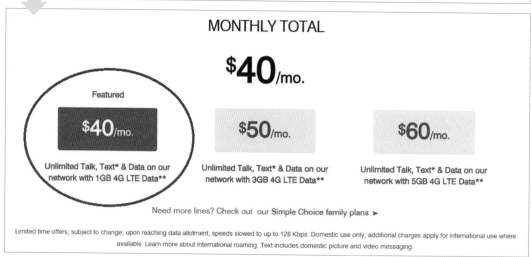

....

Answer

主要差異為網路量只有 1GB 4G LTE data。其他差異如：1GB 用完後，速度會降至 128 Kbps；使用 Music Freedom™，不占網路流量下載音樂；美國打至加拿大和墨西哥通話免費。

另外還有一個 Pay as you go. 方案，看起來似乎也很便宜，一起瞧瞧。

Pay as you go.

$3/mo.

Get any combination of 30 minutes of talk or 30 texts.

Want more? No problem.

Add additional talk and text at a low flat rate of 10 cents per minute/message (sending and receiving).

Add a high-speed data pass.

Need high-speed data? Our flexible passes will keep you streaming and downloading at 4G LTE speeds, plus each pass includes Smartphone Mobile HotSpot.

$5/day

Daily pass—up to 500MB 4G LTE data

$10/week

Weekly pass—up to 1GB of 4G LTE data

根據上圖資訊，請將此方案內容填入下表。

Pay as you go.	
Price of the plan	1
Length of the plan	2
Minutes of talk / minutes of text messages	3
Additional talk and text	4
Add a high-speed data daily pass	5
Add a high-speed data weekly pass	6

Ch
10

....

Answer

1 $3/month   2 one month   3 any combination of 30 minutes of talk or 30 texts

4 10 cents per minute/message (sending and receiving) 在美國傳送和接收簡訊或通話都是要付費的。

5 $5 per day   6 $10 per week

✏ Exercise 3

身為國際學生，Carrie 希望方案裡可以包含國際通話。$50/mo 的預付卡方案說明中，還提供了下列兩種加購方案，想打回台灣 (Taiwan) 的 Carrie 該選哪個比較划算呢？點進去查查看費率吧！

Add additional features.

Select which features you'd like to add and we'll factor the cost into your monthly estimate.

Stateside international talk

$10 ⊕ ADD

With our Simple Choice plan, calling friends and family abroad from the U.S., Mexico, and Canada is easier than ever with our Stateside International Talk service options

- Unlimited calls to landlines in 70+ countries
- $0.20/min calls to mobile numbers in 100+ countries
- Discounted rates to the rest of the world

Check rates ►

Stateside international talk

$15 ⊕ ADD

- Everything you get for $10
- Plus, unlimited calls to mobile numbers in 30+ countries

Check rates ►

<Website> http://prepaid-phones.t-mobile.com/simple-choice-prepaid-plans

✏ Exercise 4

根據點入的網頁資訊，上題兩種方案用來比較的特點，你知道各代表什麼意思嗎？

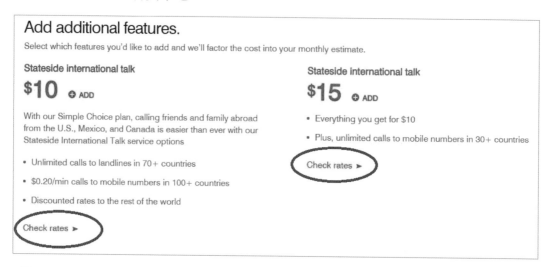

Talk all you want with unlimited calling to landlines in Taiwan.

	Mobile-to-Landline	Mobile-to-Mobile	Text (SMS)	
$15/mo per line	✓ Unlimited	$0.18/min	✓ Unlimited	With unlimited mobile-to-mobile calling unavailable to this country, this may be your best value if you plan to call any of the 30+ countries that qualify for unlimited mobile-to-mobile.
$10/mo per line	✓ Unlimited	$0.18/min	✓ Unlimited	Get **unlimited calling** to landlines and **discounted calling** to mobile numbers. See what other 70+ countries qualify.
Pay Per Use	$1.99/min	$1.99/min	✓ Unlimited*	SHOP PLANS

※ 本頁練習的答案在第 186 頁。

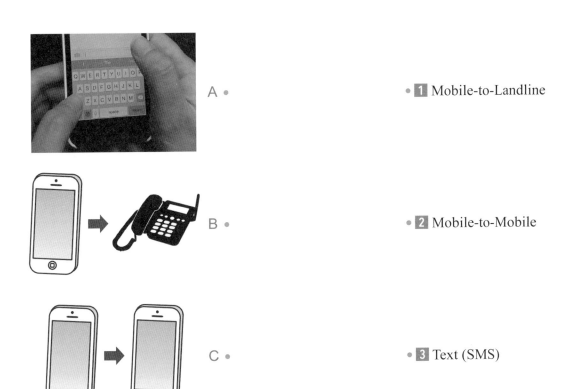

A •

• **1** Mobile-to-Landline

B •

• **2** Mobile-to-Mobile

C •

• **3** Text (SMS)

Answer Exercise 3

點選 "Check rates" 後看到 Enter the country you're calling from the U.S., Mexico or Canada. ，於欄位中填入 Taiwan。結果兩種方案打回台灣沒有差別，所以選 $10 比較划算。

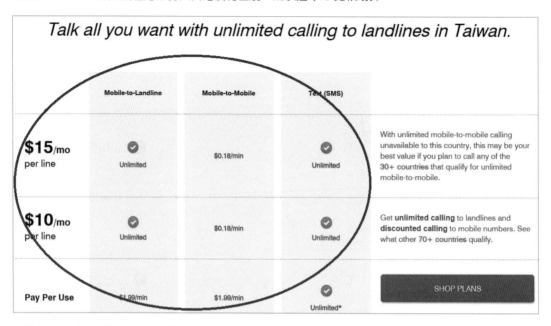

<Website> http://www.t-mobile.com/optional-services/international-calling.html?icid=WMD_PD_STTSDSCNA_8IM5UK10BPB2650#check-rates

Answer Exercise 4

1 手機打市話 = B   2 手機打手機 = C   3 傳送簡訊 = A

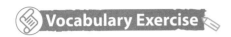

Task 1 Crossword Puzzle 填字遊戲

請根據下列英文提示，將該單字填入空格中。Hint: 可參考前面的 Key Words 表。

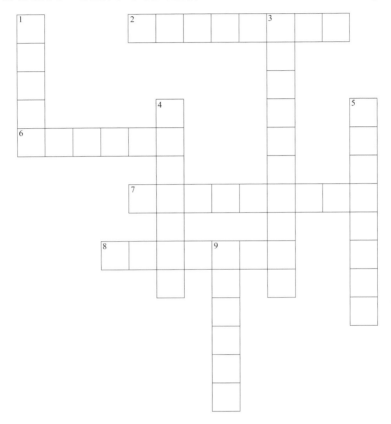

Across:

2. to set apart and give out to particular people

6. a machine or equipment invented for a particular job

7. an additional amount of money added to the usual price

8. a supply of goods or services that exceeds a preset limit

Down:

1. the rate that something moves

3. connected or related to a particular subject, activity etc.

4. to make smaller in size, number or degree

5. within one's own country

9. the total number or quantity

Answer

1. speed   2. allocate   3. associated   4. reduced   5. domestic

6. device   7. surcharge   8. overage   9. amount

Ch
10

Task 2 Scrambled Words 字母重組

請將左方亂序的字母重組成有意義的單字，最後再將各個數字裡的字母填入最後一欄。

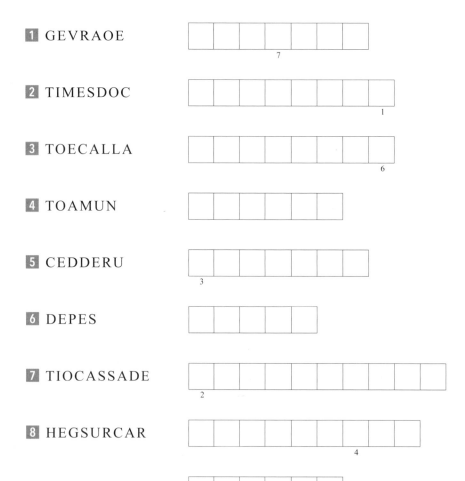

1 GEVRAOE

2 TIMESDOC

3 TOECALLA

4 TOAMUN

5 CEDDERU

6 DEPES

7 TIOCASSADE

8 HEGSURCAR

9 DEVCIE

......

 Google cell phone carriers' websites and then enter those websites.
搜尋線上手機電信公司，然後進入網站。

↓

 Look for the plan that matches your current needs.
找尋適合你目前需求的方案。

★ 多數的電信公司皆分為須綁約的 contract plans 和預付卡型的 prepaid plans。

↓

 Consider these factors when choosing a phone plan:
選擇方案時會考慮的因素：

- **Price per month** 月費
- **Number of texts** 簡訊數
- **Contract period** 合約期
- **Number of lines** 共用方案門號數
- **Number of minutes** 分鐘數
- **Amount of total data** 上網量

↓

 Get to know what is included in a prepaid monthly plan.
了解預付卡月費方案的內容。

★ 可自由選擇要購買新機或使用自己原有的手機，後者單獨購買 SIM 卡即可。

↓

Get to know other prepaid plans and international calling rates.
了解其他預付卡方案的內容以及國際通話費率。

★ 假如通話量較少，可選擇通話分鐘數有限定的方案，不過必須注意美國是接聽和撥出都要收費。

Ch
10

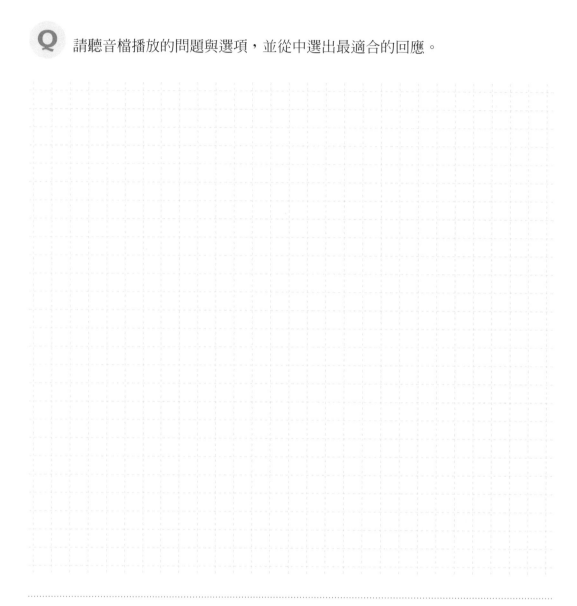

Q 請聽音檔播放的問題與選項，並從中選出最適合的回應。

Script

Hi, I'd like to cancel my current phone service next month. Is there a termination fee?

A. Yes, we'll terminate your call next month.

B. Yes, you'll have to pay $200 as it's a one-year contract.

C. How much do I owe you?

Answer B

附錄

★ 詞性註記說明:

n. = 名詞　　v. = 動詞　　a. = 形容詞　　adv. = 副詞　　prep. = 介系詞　　abbr. = 縮寫　　— = 片語、其他

1 人事與組織

單字・片語	詞性	中文
ability	n.	能力
accomplishment	n.	成就
acquire	v.	獲得
administrator	n.	管理人
aggressive	a.	有進取心的;有幹勁的
allowance	n.	津貼;限額
ambitious	a.	有野心的
applicable	a.	可實施的;可適用的
application	n.	適用
apply for	—	申請
apprentice	n.	學徒;見習生
assignment	n.	任務;工作
assistance	n.	協助
assistant	n.	助理;助教
background	n.	背景
benefit	n.	利益;好處
bonus	n.	獎金;額外津貼
boss	n.	老闆
candidate	n.	候選人;候補者
capable	a.	有能力的;能幹的
career	n.	職業
celebrate	v.	慶祝
CEO	n.	執行長;總裁
certificate	n.	證明書;執照

challenge	v.	挑戰
chief	n.	首領;長官
communication	n.	溝通
compensate	v.	補償;賠償
compensation	n.	補償;賠償
competent	a.	能幹的;稱職的
concern	n.	關心的事;擔心
confident	a.	有自信的
congratulations	n.	恭喜
consider	v.	考慮;認為
consultant	n.	顧問
contest	n.	競爭;競賽
coworker	n.	同事
deadline	n.	最後期限
deal with	—	處理;對待
debt	n.	債;借款
decrease	v.	減少;減小
deputy manager	—	副理
description	n.	敘述;形容
designate	v.	標出;指定
devote	v.	奉獻;專心於
duty	n.	責任;義務
earn	v.	賺得;贏得
earnings	n.	收入;工資
education	n.	教育
efficiency	n.	效率;功效
efficient	a.	效率高的

effort	*n.*	努力
elect	*v.*	選舉
employ	*v.*	雇用
employee	*n.*	受雇者;員工
employer	*n.*	雇主;雇用者
employment	*n.*	雇用;受雇
endurance	*n.*	忍耐;耐久力
enthusiasm	*n.*	熱心;熱誠
entire	*a.*	全部的;整個的
errand	*n.*	差事;任務
excellent	*a.*	出色的;傑出的
executive	*a.*	執行的;管理的
experience	*n.*	經驗
expert	*n.*	專家
expertise	*n.*	專門知識/技術
faculty	*n.*	師資陣容; 全體職員
fire	*v.*	解雇
fit	*v.*	使適合;使勝任
flexible	*a.*	能變通的; 有彈性的
former	*a.*	從前的;早前的
general manager	—	總經理
government	*n.*	政府;內閣
hard-working	*a.*	努力工作的; 勤勉的
hire	*v.*	租借;雇用
impressive	*a.*	給人深刻印象的; 感人的
in charge	—	負責
income	*n.*	收入;收益
incompetent	*a.*	無能力的; 不能勝任的
increase	*v.*	增大;增加
instead	*adv.*	作為替代;反而

interview	*n.*	面試;採訪
interviewee	*n.*	被面試者;受訪者
interviewer	*n.*	面試者;採訪者
job hunter	—	求職者
labor	*n.*	勞工
leader	*n.*	領袖;領導者
leadership	*n.*	領導者的地位; 領導才能
license	*n.*	許可;執照
manager	*n.*	經理
newcomer	*n.*	新來的人
nominate	*v.*	提名;任命
obtain	*v.*	得到;獲得
occupy	*v.*	占領;占據
opening	*n.*	開始;開頭
outstanding	*a.*	突出的;顯著的
pay	*v.*	支付
peer	*n.*	(地位、能力等) 同等的人;同輩
pension	*n.*	退休金;養老金
personnel	*n.*	(總稱)人員; 員工
portfolio	*n.*	文件夾;作品集
position	*n.*	位置;職位
post	*n.*	崗位;職位
president	*n.*	總統;總裁
probation	*n.*	檢驗;鑑定
profession	*n.*	職業;同行
profile	*n.*	人物簡介;概況
promising	*a.*	有希望的; 有前途的
promote	*v.*	晉升;促進
promotion	*n.*	升遷;晉級
pursue	*v.*	追趕;追蹤

qualification	*n.*	資格；能力
qualified	*a.*	具備必要條件的；合格的
quit	*v.*	離開；退出
raise	*v.*	舉起；提高
recommend	*v.*	推薦；介紹
recruit	*v.*	徵募（新成員）
recruiter	*n.*	招聘人員
reduce	*v.*	減少；縮小
reduction	*n.*	減少；削減
reference	*n.*	提及；參考
reject	*v.*	拒絕；抵制
reliable	*a.*	可靠的
reputation	*n.*	名譽；名聲
require	*v.*	需要
requirement	*n.*	需要；必須品
resign	*v.*	放棄；辭去
resignation	*n.*	辭職；放棄
respect	*n.*	敬重；尊敬
responsibility	*n.*	責任；責任感
resume	*n.*	履歷
retire	*v.*	（使）退休
reward	*n.*	報答；報償
salary	*n.*	薪資；薪水
salesperson	*n.*	店員；售貨員
satisfy	*v.*	使滿意；使高興
secretary	*n.*	祕書
seek	*v.*	尋找；探索
senior	*a.*	年長的；資深的
skill	*n.*	技能；技巧
sufficient	*a.*	足夠的；充分的
supervisor	*n.*	主管
switch	*n.*	開關
task	*n.*	任務；工作

trainer	*n.*	訓練人；教練員
training	*n.*	訓練；鍛鍊
transfer	*v.*	轉調
typist	*n.*	打字員
vice president	—	副總統；副總裁
vote	*n./v.*	投票
wages	*n.*	薪資
wealthy	*a.*	富有的
weekday	*n.*	平日；工作日
weekend	*n.*	週末
welfare	*n.*	福利
worker	*n.*	工人；勞工
workforce	*n.*	勞動力
workplace	*n.*	工作場所

2 辦公與文書

單字・片語	詞性	中文
academic	*n.*	學術的
accent	*n.*	重音；口音
access	*n.*	接近；進入
accurately	*adv.*	準確地；精確地
acquaint	*v.*	使認識；介紹
address	*n.*	住址；地址
administration	*n.*	管理；經營
adopt	*v.*	採取；採納
advance	*v.*	促進；將……提前
advice	*n.*	勸告；忠告
afterward	*adv*	之後；以後
against	*prep.*	反對；違反
agenda	*n.*	議程
air conditioner	—	空調；冷氣機
airmail	*n.*	航空郵件
allocate	*v.*	分配；分派

allocation	*n.*	分配；分派
allow	*v.*	允許；准許
alternative	*n.*	選擇；二擇一
announce	*v.*	宣布；發布
announcement	*n.*	通告；布告
applause	*n.*	鼓掌歡迎；喝采
appointment	*n.*	會面；約定
archives	*n.*	檔案；文件
arrange	*v.*	整理；安排
arrangement	*n.*	安排；準備工作
aspect	*n.*	方面；觀點
assemble	*v.*	集合；召集
attach	*v.*	裝上；附加
attachment	*n.*	連接；附件
attend	*v.*	出席；參加
attention	*n.*	注意；注意力
attn	*abbr.*	敬請知悉
available	*a.*	可用的
avenue	*n.*	大街；大道
block	*n.*	街區
board	*n.*	木板；版
branch	*n.*	分公司；分店
brief	*a.*	簡短的
briefing	*n.*	簡報
browse	*v.*	瀏覽
bulletin board	—	布告欄
business card	—	名片
cabinet	*n.*	櫥；櫃
calculator	*n.*	計算機
call	*v.*	打電話
caller	*n.*	打電話者
campaign	*n.*	活動
capacity	*n.*	容量；容積

cart	*n.*	手推車
carton	*n.*	紙盒；紙箱
cartridge	*n.*	筆芯
case	*n.*	箱；盒
categorize	*v.*	將……分類
caution	*n.*	小心；謹慎
cell phone	—	行動電話；手機
center	*n.*	中心；中央
chairperson	*n.*	主席；議長
chamber	*n.*	會議廳
chart	*n.*	圖；圖表
clipboard	*n.*	附有紙夾的筆記板
clock in	—	打卡上班
clock out	—	打卡下班
code	*n.*	代號；密碼
colleague	*n.*	同事
collect	*v.*	收集；採集
comment	*n./v.*	評論
committee	*n.*	委員會
company	*n.*	公司；商號
compliance	*n.*	承諾；遵循
comprehensive	*a.*	廣泛的；有充分理解力的
computer	*n.*	電腦
conclusion	*n.*	結論；推論
concur	*v.*	同意；合作
conduct	*v.*	引領；帶領
confer	*v.*	授予（學位等）
conference	*n.*	會議；討論會
conference room	—	會議室
congress	*n.*	會議；代表大會
connection	*n.*	連接；聯絡
consecutive	*a.*	連續不斷的
consensus	*n.*	一致；合意

conservative	*a.*	保守的;守舊的
constructive	*a.*	建設性的;積極的
contact	*n.*	接觸;觸碰
control	*v.*	控制;支配
convention	*n.*	會議;大會
convince	*v.*	使確信;使信服
copier	*n.*	影印機
copy	*n.*	抄本;副本
cord	*n.*	絕緣電線
correspondence	*n.*	一致;符合
council	*n.*	會議
data	*n.*	資料;數據
database	*n.*	資料庫;數據庫
date	*n.*	日期;日子
debate	*n.*	辯論;討論
decision	*n.*	決定;決心
declaration	*n.*	宣布;宣告
delegate	*v.*	委派……為代表
department	*n.*	部門
detach	*v.*	分開;拆卸
dial	*v.*	打電話
digital	*a.*	數位的
directory	*n.*	工商名錄
disapproval	*n.*	不贊成;非難
discipline	*n.*	紀律;風紀
discuss	*v.*	討論;商談
disk	*n.*	光碟;磁碟
disposal	*n.*	處理;處置
division	*n.*	分開;分割
documentary	*n.*	紀錄片
download	*v.*	(電腦)下載
election	*n.*	選舉;當選
email	*n.*	電子郵件

enclose	*v.*	把(公文、票據等)封入
enforce	*v.*	實施;執行
engineer	*n.*	工程師;技師
enhance	*v.*	提高;增加(價值、品質等)
enroll	*v.*	把……記入名冊;登記(名字等)
enrollment	*n.*	登記;入會
envelope	*n.*	信封
environment	*n.*	環境;四周狀況
equipment	*n.*	配備;裝備
eraser	*n.*	板擦;橡皮擦
establish	*v.*	建立;設立
estate	*n.*	地產;財產
execute	*v.*	實施;實行
executive	*a.*	執行的;實施的
exit	*n.*	出口;通道
expansion	*n.*	擴展;擴張
extension number	—	分機號碼
external	*a.*	外面的;外部的
facility	*n.*	能力;技能
fax	*n.*	傳真
feedback	*n.*	意見回饋
file	*n.*	文件
fix	*v.*	使固定;釘牢
focus	*n.*	焦點;焦距
folder	*n.*	文書夾;紙夾
formal	*a.*	正式的
forward	*adv.*	向前;向將來
furnish	*v.*	為……配備傢俱;提供
furniture	*n.*	傢俱
guidance	*n.*	指導;輔導

hardware	*n.*	（電腦）硬體
highlight	*n.*	最突出／最精采的部分
	v.	強調
implement	*n.*	工具；器具
	v.	執行；實施
in regard to	—	關於
incoming	*n.*	收入
incorporation	*n.*	合併；編入
information	*n.*	資訊；消息
in-house	*a.*	機構內的；公司內部的
inquire	*v.*	詢問
install	*v.*	安裝；設置
instruction	*n.*	使用說明
internal	*a.*	內部的
internet	*n.*	網路
interrupted	*a.*	中斷的
introduction	*n.*	介紹；正式引見
issue	*v.*	發行；發布
item	*n.*	項目；品項
laptop	*n.*	筆記型電腦
layout	*n.*	安排；設計
leave a message	—	留言；留話
lecture	*n.*	授課；演講
lecturer	*n.*	講演者
letter	*n.*	信；函件
letterhead	*n.*	信頭；印有信頭的信紙
link	*v.*	連結
list	*n.*	表；名冊
local	*a.*	當地的
login	*v.*	（電腦）登入
logo	*n.*	標誌；商標

lunch meeting	—	午餐會議
machine	*n.*	機器；機械
mail	*n.*	郵件
manual	*n.*	使用手冊
marker	*n.*	馬克筆
material	*n.*	材料；資料
meeting	*n.*	會議；集會
meeting room	—	會議室
memo	*n.*	備忘錄；便條
memorize	*v.*	記住；背熟
mention	*v.*	提到；說起
message	*n.*	訊息；留言
minutes	*n.*	會議紀錄
monitor	*n.*	監視／聽器
network	*n.*	網絡
note	*n.*	筆記；紀錄
notice	*n.*	公告；通知
objection	*n.*	反對；異議
office	*n.*	辦公室
office supplies	—	辦公用品
online	*a.*	線上的
operation	*n.*	操作；運轉
opinion	*n.*	意見；見解
opposition	*n.*	反對；反抗
option	*n.*	選擇；選擇權
orientation	*n.*	定位；方向
output	*n.*	產量；（電腦）輸出
panel	*n.*	控制板；配電盤
paperwork	*n.*	日常文書工作
part	*n.*	（一）部分
participant	*n.*	關係者；參與者
partition	*n.*	分開；分割
password	*n.*	密碼

path	*n.*	小徑;路徑
permission	*n.*	允許;許可
perspective	*n.*	觀點;洞察力
phone number	—	電話號碼
photocopy	*v.*	影印
placement	*n.*	布置;人員配置
plug	*n.*	插頭
policy	*n.*	政策;方針
postal	*a.*	郵政的;郵局的
postpone	*v.*	使延期;延遲
precise	*a.*	精確的;準確的
presence	*n.*	出席;在場
present	*a.*	出席的;在場的
presentation	*n.*	簡報
principle	*n.*	原則;原理
print	*v.*	印;印刷
printer	*n.*	印表機
priority	*n.*	優先
privacy	*n.*	隱私;私事
procedure	*n.*	程序;手續
proceed	*v.*	繼續進行; 繼續做 / 講下去
process	*n.*	過程;進程
processor	*n.*	加工者;製造者
projector	*n.*	投影機
propose	*v.*	提議;建議
protect	*v.*	保護;防護
purpose	*n.*	目的;意圖
reaffirm	*v.*	重申
rearrange	*v.*	重新安排
receive	*v.*	收到;接到
recognize	*v.*	認出;識別
recycle	*v.*	再利用
refer to	—	提到;談論

reform	*v.*	改革;革新
remain	*v.*	剩下;餘留
reminder	*n.*	提醒者;提醒物
replace	*v.*	把……放回(原處)
reply	*n./v.*	回答;答覆
report	*n./v.*	報告;報導
reschedule	*v.*	重新安排時間
resource	*n.*	資源;物力
respond	*v.*	回答;作出反應
response	*n.*	回答;答覆
restriction	*n.*	限制;約束
rule	*n.*	規則;規定
run	*v.*	跑;奔
scan	*v.*	掃描
scanner	*n.*	掃描器
screen	*n.*	螢幕
search	*v.*	搜尋
second	*a.*	第二(次)的
security	*n.*	安全;安全感
seminar	*n.*	研討會
session	*n.*	會議
significant	*a.*	有意義的;重大的
software	*n.*	(電腦)軟體
solution	*n.*	解答;解決辦法
speaker	*n.*	說話者;擴音器
speech	*n.*	演講
spokesperson	*n.*	發言人
staff	*n.*	(全體)職員; 工作人員
staircase	*n.*	樓梯;樓梯間
stamp	*n.*	郵票
statement	*n.*	陳述;說明
stationery	*n.*	文具;信紙

subject	n.	主題；題目
subscribe	v.	訂閱
subsidiary	a.	輔助的；附帶的
substitute	n.	代替人；代替物
summary	n.	總結；摘要
supervise	v.	監督；管理
supervision	n.	管理；監督
system	n.	體系；系統
take place	—	舉行；發生
team	n.	隊；組
technique	n.	技巧；技術
teleconference	n.	電信會議
text	n.	正文；文本
time clock	—	打卡鐘
topic	n.	題目；話題
trainee	n.	練習生；受訓者
transaction	n.	辦理；處置
troubleshooting	n.	疑難排解
turn down	—	拒絕
update	v.	更新
upgrade	v.	升級
valuate	v.	對……作估價
videoconference	n.	視訊會議
viewpoint	n.	觀點；見解
voicemail	n.	語音信箱
website	n.	網站
whiteboard	n.	白板
workshop	n.	工作坊；研討會

3 出差

單字・片語	詞性	中文
A.M.	abbr.	上午
abroad	adv.	在國外；到國外

accelerate	v.	使增速；促使
accident	n.	意外
accommodation	n.	住處
accuse	v.	指責；歸咎
airfare	n.	飛機票價
airline	n.	（飛機的）航線；航空公司
airplane	n.	飛機
airport	n.	機場
aisle seat	—	靠走道的座位
alert	n.	警戒；警報
altitude	n.	高；高度
apologize	v.	道歉；認錯
approximate	a.	近似的；接近的
argue	v.	爭論；辯論
arrival time	—	到達時間
arrive	v.	到達；到來
automobile	n.	汽車
baggage	n.	行李
baggage claim area	—	行李認領區
bathroom	n.	浴室
bedroom	n.	臥室；寢室
bellhop	n.	旅館服務生
belongings	n.	財產；攜帶物品
board	v.	登機
boarding	n.	登機
boarding pass	—	登機證
book	v.	預訂；預約
booking	n.	預訂；預約
brake	n.	煞車
broadcast	v.	廣播；播送
business class	—	商務艙
business trip	—	出差

cancel	v.	取消
captain	n.	機長
baggage carousel	—	行李輸送帶
chain	n.	連鎖店
cheap	a.	便宜的；價廉的
check-in	n.	機場報到；登記住房
check-out	n.	退房；結帳離開
choice	n.	選擇；抉擇
clear	a.	清楚的；透明的
clearance	n.	清倉大拍賣
climb	v.	爬；攀登
clock	n.	時鐘
cloudy	a.	多雲的；陰天的
commute	v.	通勤
commuter	n.	通勤者
complain	v.	抱怨；發牢騷
confirm	v.	證實；確定
confirmation	n.	確定；確證
congestion	n.	擁塞；擠滿
connecting flight	—	中轉航班
convey	v.	運輸；傳遞
credit card	—	信用卡
crew	n.	全體機組人員
cruise	v.	緩慢巡行；漫遊
customer	n.	顧客
customs	n.	關稅
damage	n.	損害；損失
dangerous	a.	危險的
delay	v.	延緩；使延期
departure	n.	離開；出發
departure time	—	起飛時間
destination	n.	目的地；終點
direction	n.	方向；方位

distance	n.	距離；路程
domestic flight	—	國內航班
driver	n.	駕駛員；司機
early	a.	早的；提早的
	adv.	早一點；提早
economy class	—	經濟艙
engine	n.	發動機；引擎
entrance	n.	入口；門口
exchange rate	—	匯率
expense	n.	費用；價錢
expensive	a.	高貴的；昂貴的
fare	n.	（交通工具的）票價；車／船費
fee	n.	費用（如學費、入場費等）
ferry	n.	渡輪
fill out	—	填寫
first class	—	頭等艙
flight	n.	航班
flight attendant	—	空服人員
front desk	—	櫃台
fuel	n.	燃料
gasoline	n.	汽油
gate	n.	大門
guest	n.	客人；賓客
guide	n.	嚮導；導遊
	v.	帶領；引導
handbook	n.	手冊
harbor	n.	港灣；海港
highway	n.	公路；幹道
hostel	n.	旅舍（尤指青年旅社）
hotel	n.	旅館；飯店

inexpensive	*a.*	花費不多的；價錢低廉的
insurance	*n.*	保險
international flight	—	國際航班
itinerary	*n.*	旅程；路線
journey	*n.*	旅行
kilogram	*n.*	公斤
kilometer	*n.*	公里
landing	*n.*	降落
late	*a.*	遲的；晚的
leave for	—	（離開某地）到某地去
lobby	*n.*	大廳
lodging	*n.*	借宿；住所
lost-and-found	—	失物招領處
luggage	*n.*	行李
mile	*n.*	英里；哩
minute	*n.*	分（鐘）
MRT	*n.*	大眾捷運系統
o'clock	*adv.*	……點鐘
on holiday	—	在休假中
on time	—	準時
overbook	*v.*	超訂
P.M.	*abbr.*	下午
park	*n.*	公園；遊樂場
	v.	停車
parking lot	—	停車場
pass	*n.*	通行證；及格
	v.	前進；通過
passenger	*n.*	乘客；旅客
passport	*n.*	護照；通行證
permit	*v.*	允許；許可
pilot	*n.*	駕駛員
platform	*n.*	月台

port	*n.*	港口
price	*n.*	價格；價錢
prior to	—	在……之前；首要
procrastinate	*v.*	延遲；耽擱
punctual	*a.*	準時的
queue	*n.*	（人或車輛等的）行列；長隊
railroad	*n.*	鐵路
reception	*n.*	接待；接見
receptionist	*n.*	接待員；傳達員
reservation	*n.*	預訂
resort	*n.*	度假名勝
room service	—	客房服務
route	*n.*	路；路線
rush hour	—	交通尖峰時間
seat belt	—	安全帶
shuttle bus	—	區間車；接駁車
signal	*n.*	信號；暗號
station	*n.*	車站
stay	*n./v.*	停留；留下
steer	*v.*	掌（船）舵；駕駛
suitcase	*n.*	小型旅行箱；手提箱
suite	*n.*	套房
terminal	*n.*	航廈；總站
timetable	*n.*	時刻表
tour	*n.*	旅行；旅遊
tourism	*n.*	旅遊；觀光
tourist	*n.*	旅遊者；觀光者
traffic jam	—	塞車
transfer	*v.*	轉車
transit	*n.*	運輸；運送
transit visa	—	過境簽證
transport	*n.*	運輸

transportation	*n.*	交通;運輸
travel	*v.*	旅行
travel agency	—	旅行社
trip	*n.*	旅行;航行
tunnel	*n.*	隧道;地道
turbulence	*n.*	亂流
vehicle	*n.*	運載工具;車輛
visit	*n./v.*	參觀;拜訪
voucher	*n.*	票券;憑證
weather	*n.*	天氣
wheel	*n.*	輪子;車輪
window seat	—	靠窗座位

4 公司不動產

單字・片語	詞性	中文
advantage	*n.*	有利條件;優點
afford	*v.*	買得起;有足夠的……(去做……)
ambulance	*n.*	救護車
apartment	*n.*	公寓
application	*n.*	應用;適用
architecture	*n.*	建築學;建築術
asset	*n.*	財產;資產
builder	*n.*	建築者;建築商
centimeter	*n.*	公分
construction	*n.*	建造;建設
contractor	*n.*	立契約者
corridor	*n.*	走廊
curtain	*n.*	簾;窗簾
deposit	*n.*	保證金;押金
destroy	*v.*	毀壞;破壞
disadvantage	*n.*	不利條件
drain	*n.*	排水管
escalator	*n.*	電扶梯

expand	*v.*	展開;擴大
facilitate	*v.*	使容易;促進
floor plan	—	建築之平面圖
flooring	*n.*	地板材料
gas	*n.*	瓦斯
heater	*n.*	加熱器;暖氣機
height	*n.*	高;高度
high-rise	*a.*	有多層的;高樓的
housing	*n.*	住房建築;住宅
interior	*a.*	內的;內部的
interior design	—	室內設計
landlord	*n.*	房東;(旅館等的)主人
landmark	*n.*	地標
leak	*n.*	漏洞;裂縫
lend	*v.*	把……借給
lighting	*n.*	照明
location	*n.*	位置;場所
measurement	*n.*	測量(法)
neighborhood	*n.*	鄰近地區
next door	—	(在)隔壁
ownership	*n.*	物主身分;所有權
period	*n.*	時期;期間
plumber	*n.*	水電工
possession	*n.*	擁有;占有
public	*a.*	公眾的
quality	*n.*	品質
rebuild	*v.*	重建;改建
relocate	*v.*	(將……)重新安置
renovation	*n.*	更新;修理
rent	*v.*	出租
rental	*n.*	租金
residence	*n.*	居住;住宅

restructuring	n.	重建；改組
steel	n.	鋼；鋼鐵
story	n.	樓層
structure	n.	結構；構造
surroundings	n.	環境；周圍的事物
tenant	n.	房客
underground	a.	地下的
utilities	n.	水電瓦斯費

5 財務與會計

單字・片語	詞性	中文
absorb	v.	合併（公司等）
accountant	n.	會計；會計師
accounting	n.	會計；會計學
accumulate	v.	累積；積聚
auction	n.	拍賣
audit	n./v.	審計；查帳
auditor	n.	查帳員；稽核員
bond	n.	債券
broker	n.	股票經紀人
check	n.	支票
checkbook	n.	支票簿
controller	n.	主計員；查帳員
conversion	n.	（證券、貨幣等的）兌換
currency	n.	通貨；貨幣
cut down	—	削減；縮短
finance	n.	財政；金融
financial	a.	財政的；金融的
figure	n.	數量；金額
fluctuate	v.	波動；變動
investor	n.	投資者；出資者
loan	n.	貸款
maximum	n.	最大量；最大數

minimum	n.	最小量；最小數
predict	v.	預言；預料
pressure	n.	壓力
real estate	—	不動產
recession	n.	（經濟的）衰退
risk	n.	危險；風險
savings	n.	儲金；存款
settlement	n.	解決；清算結帳
shares	n.	股票
slump	n.	物價下跌；經濟衰退
speculate	v.	思索；沉思
statistical	a.	統計的；統計學的
statistics	n.	統計；統計資料
stimulate	v.	刺激；激勵
stock market	—	股票市場
stockholder	n.	股東
subtotal	n.	小計
yearly	a.	每年的；一年一次的
	adv.	一年一次地

6 製造與技術

單字・片語	詞性	中文
advanced	a.	先進的
affect	v.	影響
amazing	a.	驚人的；出色的
analysis	n.	分析；分解
analyze	v.	分析
appliance	n.	器具；裝備
approach	v.	接近；靠近
artificial	a.	人工的；人造的
assemble	v.	裝配
assembly line	—	裝配線

automatic	*a.*	自動的
biology	*n.*	生物學
blackout	*n.*	停電
bleed	*v.*	出血；流血
blend	*v.*	使混合；使混雜
breed	*v.*	繁殖；育種
bulb	*n.*	燈泡
cargo	*n.*	（船、飛機、車輛裝載的）貨物
chemical	*a.*	化學的
chemist	*n.*	化學家
chemistry	*n.*	化學
chip	*n.*	晶片
competitive	*a.*	競爭的；經由競爭的
consist	*v.*	組成；構成
convenient	*a.*	方便的
device	*n.*	設備；裝置
discover	*v.*	發現
disease	*n.*	疾病
dose	*n.*	（藥物等的）一劑；一服
electric	*a.*	電的
electrician	*n.*	電工；電氣技師
finding	*n.*	發現；研究結果
fridge	*n.*	冰箱
function	*n.*	功能
gear	*n.*	設備；裝置
guideline	*n.*	指導方針
heal	*v.*	治療
inaccuracy	*n.*	不正確；不精確
industry	*n.*	工業；企業
instrument	*n.*	儀器；器具
introduce	*v.*	介紹；引見

invention	*n.*	發明；創造
journal	*n.*	雜誌；期刊
laboratory	*n.*	實驗室；研究室
machinery	*n.*	機器；機械
maintenance	*n.*	維持；保持
malfunction	*v.*	發生故障
manufacture	*v.*	製造；加工
measure	*v.*	測量；計量
mechanic	*n.*	機械工；修理工
mechanical	*a.*	機械的
medicine	*n.*	藥；內服藥
numerous	*adj.*	許多的；很多的
operate	*v.*	操作
operator	*n.*	操作者；總機；司機
organic	*adj.*	有機的
organize	*v.*	組織；安排
output	*n.*	出產；生產
overall	*n.*	工作褲
pharmacist	*n.*	藥劑師
phenomena	*n.*	現象
physician	*n.*	（內科）醫師
pioneer	*n.*	先驅
plant	*n.*	工廠
portable	*a.*	便於攜帶的；手提式的
power failure	—	電源故障／中斷
power plant	—	發電廠
practical	*a.*	實踐的；實際的
prevent	*v.*	防止；預防
prevention	*n.*	預防；防止
produce	*v.*	生產；製造
product	*n.*	產品
productive	*a.*	生產的；多產的

professional	a.	專業的
prohibit	v.	禁止
proof	n.	證據；物證
pursuit	n.	追蹤；追擊
quality control	—	品質控管
quantity	n.	量
quota	n.	配額；定額
rapidly	adv.	很快地；立即地
reaction	n.	反應；感應
recovery	n.	重獲；復得
reform	v.	改革；革新
regulate	v.	管理；控制
regulation	n.	規章；規則
remedy	n.	治療（法）
renewal	n.	更新；復原
reorganization	n.	改組；改編
repair	v.	修理；修補
repetition	n.	重複；反覆
request	n.	要求；請求
research	n.	調查；探究
researcher	n.	研究員；調查者
resolution	n.	決心；決定
resolve	v.	解決；解答
review	v.	再檢查；檢閱
revolution	n.	革命
routine	n.	例行公事；日常工作
safety	n.	安全；平安
scheme	n.	計畫；方案
scientist	n.	科學家
screening	n.	篩選；審查
selection	n.	選擇；選拔
simplify	v.	簡化；精簡
standard	n.	標準

step	n.	腳步；步驟
strict	a.	嚴格的；嚴厲的
systematic	a.	有系統的
technical	a.	技術的
technician	n.	技術人員；技師
telecommunication	n.	電信
telegram	n.	電報
therapy	n.	療法
tool	n.	工具
turn off	—	關掉（電器）
turn on	—	打開（電器）
warranty	n.	保固
wire	n.	電線
workload	n.	工作量

7 採購與後勤

單字・片語	詞性	中文
approve	v.	贊成；批准
bargain	v.	討價還價
bid	v.	喊價
bill of lading	—	提貨單
brand-new	a.	全新的
breakdown	n.	（機器等的）故障；損壞
buyer	n.	採購者；買家
by air	—	搭飛機
by water	—	乘船
carriage	n.	運費
cash	n.	現金；現款
catalog	n.	型錄
certificate	n.	證明書；執照
charge	v.	索價；對……索費
commodity	n.	商品；日用品
coupon	n.	折價券；配給券

courier	*n.*	快遞員;快遞公司
coverage	*n.*	覆蓋;涵蓋範圍
cracked	*a.*	破裂的;碎的
dealer	*n.*	業者;商人
deliver	*v.*	投遞;傳送
discount	*n.*	折扣
exemption	*n.*	(義務等的) 免除;免(稅)
export	*v.*	輸出;出品
freight	*n.*	運費;貨運
import	*n.*	進口;輸入
in stock	—	有現貨或存貨
invoice	*n.*	發票;發貨單
merchandise	*n.*	商品;貨物
on sale	—	上市的;出售的
order	*n.*	訂單;訂貨
origin	*n.*	起源;由來
out of stock	—	無庫存
overweight	*a.*	超重的;過重的
owe	*v.*	欠(債等)
package	*n.*	包裹;包
parcel	*n.*	小包;包裹
payable	*a.*	應支付的;到期的
payment	*n.*	支付;付款
persuade	*v.*	說服;勸服
postage	*n.*	郵資;郵費
postal	*a.*	郵政的;郵局的
postmark	*n.*	郵戳
prepay	*v.*	預付;提前繳納
price	*n.*	價格;價錢
procurement	*n.*	採購;取得
purchase	*v.*	購買
rebate	*n.*	折扣;貼現
receipt	*n.*	收據

receiver	*n.*	受領人;收件人
refund	*n.*	退還;退款
refundable	*a.*	可退還的; 可退款的
refuse	*v.*	拒絕;拒受
reimburse	*v.*	償還;退還
reimbursement	*n.*	償還;退還
retail	*n.*	零售
retailer	*n.*	零售商;零售店
return	*n.*	報酬;退貨
second-hand	*a.*	二手的;中古的
secure	*a.*	安全的
seller	*n.*	銷售者;賣方
ship	*v.*	運送;郵寄
shipment	*n.*	裝運;裝載的貨物
shipper	*n.*	託運人;貨主
shopkeeper	*n.*	店主;商店經理
shopping	*n.*	購物
stock	*n.*	進貨;庫存
storage	*n.*	貯藏;保管
supplier	*n.*	供應商
supply	*v.*	供給;供應
tracking number	—	追蹤編號
trader	*n.*	商人;商船
trunk	*n.*	後車廂
unload	*v.*	(卸)貨/客
unpack	*v.*	打開(包裹等) 取出東西
unsecured	*a.*	無擔保的; 不穩固的
urgent	*a.*	緊急的;急迫的
variety	*n.*	多樣化;變化
various	*a.*	各式各樣的
vend	*v.*	出售;販賣

單字・片語	詞性	中文
via	prep.	經由
warehouse	n.	倉庫；貨棧
worldwide	a.	遍及全球的
wrap	v.	包；裹
x-ray	n.	X 光

8 娛樂與交際

單字・片語	詞性	中文
acquaintance	n.	（與人）相識；熟人
amusement	n.	樂趣；娛樂
ancestor	n.	祖宗；祖先
ancient	a.	古代的
antique	n.	古董
appetite	n.	食慾；胃口
appetizer	n.	開胃菜
appraisal	n.	評價
appreciation	n.	欣賞；鑑賞
artist	n.	藝術家；美術家
artistic	a.	藝術的；美術的
attractive	a.	有吸引力的；引人注目的
audience	n.	聽眾；觀眾
audio	n.	（電視等的）音響裝置
audiovisual	a.	視聽的
auditorium	n.	聽眾席；觀眾席
bake	v.	烘；烤
ballroom	n.	宴會廳
banquet	n.	宴會；盛宴
bar	n.	酒吧
beverage	n.	飲料
booklet	n.	小冊子
brunch	n.	早午餐

單字・片語	詞性	中文
buffet	n.	吃到飽自助餐
cafeteria	n.	自助餐廳／食堂
cater	v.	提供飲食；承辦宴席
check	n.	（餐廳的）帳單
chef	n.	主廚
chopstick	n.	筷子
cocktail	n.	雞尾酒
compose	v.	作（詩、曲等）；構（圖）
concert	n.	音樂會；演唱會
concert hall	—	音樂廳
cook	v.	烹調；煮
cooker	n.	炊具；烹調器具
cooking	n.	烹調；烹調術
delicate	a.	易碎的
designer	n.	設計者；構思者
dessert	n.	甜點
digest	v.	消化（食物）
dining	n.	進餐
distinguish	v.	區別；識別
drama	n.	戲劇
drinks	n.	飲料
drunk	a.	喝醉（酒）的
entertainer	n.	請客者；表演者
entrée	n.	主菜
etiquette	n.	禮節；禮儀
exhibition	n.	展覽；展覽會
film	n.	底片
filmmaker	n.	影片製作人及導演等
gallery	n.	畫廊；美術館
gourmet	n.	美食家

headphone / headset	*n.*	頭戴式耳機（常複數）
historian	*n.*	歷史學家
ingredient	*n.*	（烹調的）原料
inspire	*v.*	鼓舞；激勵
invitation	*n.*	邀請；請帖
invite	*v.*	邀請；招待
juicy	*a.*	多汁的
ketchup	*n.*	番茄醬
leisure	*n.*	閒暇；空暇時間
liquor	*n.*	酒；含酒精飲料
luncheon	*n.*	午餐；（正式的）午餐會
manners	*n.*	禮貌；規矩
meal	*n.*	膳食；一餐
mean	*a.*	吝嗇的；小氣的
menu	*n.*	菜單
microphone	*n.*	麥克風
museum	*n.*	博物館
musician	*n.*	音樂家
opera	*n.*	歌劇
orchestra	*n.*	管弦樂隊
original	*a.*	最初的；本來的
perform	*v.*	執行；演出
performance	*n.*	表演
performer	*n.*	演出者；演奏者
philosopher	*n.*	哲學家；思想家
photo	*n.*	照片
photograph	*n.*	照片
photographer	*n.*	攝影師；照相師
pianist	*n.*	鋼琴家；鋼琴演奏者
pirate	*n.*	海盜；盜版者
poster	*n.*	海報

premiere	*v.*	首映
preview	*n.*	試映；預告片
recipe	*n.*	食譜
recreation	*n.*	消遣；娛樂
rehearsal	*n.*	排練；彩排
relax	*v.*	放鬆
release	*n./v.*	發行；發表
roast	*v.*	烤；炙
rotten	*a.*	腐爛的
sauce	*n.*	調味醬；醬汁
sculpture	*n.*	雕刻品；雕塑品
seafood	*n.*	海鮮
serving	*n.*	服務
showroom	*n.*	展示廳；陳列室
spicy	*a.*	加有香料的；辣的
stadium	*n.*	體育場；運動場
statue	*n.*	雕像；塑像
studio	*n.*	（畫家等的）工作室；畫室
tablecloth	*n.*	桌布
take away	—	拿走；帶走
tasty	*a.*	美味的
theater	*n.*	劇場；電影院
tip	*n.*	小費
tissue	*n.*	餐巾；面紙
tray	*n.*	盤子；托盤
utensil	*n.*	器皿；用具
vegetarian	*a.*	素食主義者的；吃素的
violinist	*n.*	小提琴手
waiter	*n.*	（男）侍者；服務生
waitress	*n.*	女服務生

9 業務與企劃

單字・片語	詞性	中文
advertise	v.	作廣告／宣傳
advertisement	n.	廣告；宣傳
advertiser	n.	刊登廣告者；廣告客戶
ambassador	n.	大使；使節
anticipate	v.	預期；期望
approximate	a.	近似的；接近的
article	n.	物品；商品
assessment	n.	估價；評估
author	n.	作者；作家
average	n.	平均；平均數
biography	n.	傳記
boost	n.	推動；為……作宣傳
brand	n.	商標；品牌
brochure	n.	小冊子
budget	n.	預算
build	v.	建築；造
business	n.	生意；營業
businessperson	n.	商人
case	n.	事例；案子
celebrity	n.	名人；名流
circumstance	n.	情況；環境
close down	—	停業
collaborate	v.	共同工作；合作
column	n.	專欄
columnist	n.	專欄作家
commentary	n.	評論
commerce	n.	商業；貿易
commercial	a.	商業的；商務的
compete	v.	競爭；對抗
competition	n.	競爭；角逐

單字・片語	詞性	中文
competitor	n.	競爭者；對手
compose	v.	排字；排版
conduct	v.	引導；帶領
consequently	adv.	結果；因此
considerable	a.	相當大／多的
consumer	n.	消費者；消耗者
contrast with	—	與……形成對比；與……相比
coordinator	n.	協調者
decade	n.	十年
decline	v.	下降；下跌
develop	v.	發展
devise	v.	設計；發明
distribution	n.	分配；銷售（量）
double	a.	兩倍的；加倍的
drop	n.	（一）滴
economic	a.	經濟上的；經濟學的
economy	n.	節約；節省
effective	a.	有效的
enlarge	v.	擴大；擴展
enterprise	n.	（有一定冒險性的）事業
estimate	v.	估計；估量
evaluate	v.	評估
evaluation	n.	評估
evolve	v.	使逐步形成；發展
exclusively	adv.	專門地；獨占地
explain	v.	解釋；說明
explode	v.	使爆炸；使爆發
express	v.	表達；陳述
factory	n.	工廠
flyer	n.	（廣告）傳單
forecast	n./v.	預測；預報

founder	v.	（計畫、事業等）失敗
franchise	n.	特權；經銷權
freelance	n.	（不受雇於人的）自由作家等
fundraiser	n.	資金籌集人／活動
fundraising	n.	募款
goal	n.	目的；目標
handle	v.	處理；對待
headline	n.	標題
headquarters	n.	總公司；總部
host	n.	主人；主持人
improve	v.	改進；改善
industrial	adj.	工業的；產業的
industry	n.	工業；企業
inflation	n.	通貨膨脹
influential	a.	有影響力的；有權勢的
initial	a.	開始的；最初的
initiate	v.	開始；創始
innovative	a.	創新的
inspection	n.	檢查；檢驗
invest	v.	投（資）；耗費
investigate	v.	調查；研究
investment	n.	投資（額）
investor	n.	投資者；出資者
journalist	n.	新聞工作者；記者
launch	v.	發起；開始從事
leaflet	n.	傳單
loss	n.	喪失；遺失
management	n.	管理；經營
market	n.	市場
marketing	n.	行銷；銷售
media	n.	大眾傳媒

merchandise	n.	商品；貨物
merger	n.	（公司等的）合併
newscaster	n.	新聞主播
newsletter	n.	業務通訊
objective	a.	客觀的
ongoing	a.	前進的；進行的
opportunity	n.	機會；良機
organization	n.	組機；機構
outlet	n.	暢貨中心
outline	n.	概要；草案
overview	n.	概觀；概要
pending	a.	未定的
percentage	n.	百分率；百分比
plan	n.	計畫；方案
planner	n.	計畫者
politician	n.	政治家
poll	n.	民意調查
possibility	n.	可能性
potential	a.	潛在的；可能的
predict	v.	預言；預料
preliminary	a.	預備的；初步的
premeditate	v.	預先考慮；預謀
preparation	n.	準備；預備
prerequisite	a.	不可缺的；事先需要的
press	v.	按；壓
primary	a.	首要的；主要的
profit	n.	利潤；盈利
profitable	a.	有利的
program	n.	節目；計畫；（電腦）程式；程式設計
programmer	n.	程式設計師
progress	v.	進行；進步

210

progression	n.	前進；發展
project	v.	計畫；企劃
proposal	n.	提案
prospect	n.	指望；預期
prospectus	n.	創辦計畫書
prosper	v.	繁榮；昌盛
prosperity	n.	繁榮；昌盛
publication	n.	出版；發行
publicity	n.	（公眾的）注意；名聲
publish	v.	出版；發行
publisher	n.	出版／發行者（公司）
quarter	n.	四分之一；季度
quarterly	a.	季度的；按季度的
	adv.	按季度地
questionnaire	n.	問卷
quote	v.	引用；引述
reach	v.	抵達；達到
remark	v.	談到；評論
reporter	n.	記者
representative	a.	代表性的；典型的
sale	n.	賣；出售
scale	n.	刻度；規模
schedule	n.	時間表；日程表
sponsor	n.	發起者；贊助者
stable	n.	穩定的
strategy	n.	戰略；策略
suggest	v.	建議；提議
survey	n./v.	調查；勘查
target	n.	目標
trend	n.	潮流；趨勢
turnover	n.	營業額；交易額
venture	n.	冒險；冒險事業

yield	n.	產量；收益

🔟 法務與稅務

單字．片語	詞性	中文
agreement	n.	協議；契約
amount	n.	總額；數量
attorney	n.	律師
authority	n.	權力；權威
authorize	v.	授權；全權委託
calculate	v.	計算；估計
citizen	n.	市民；國民
claim	n.	（根據權利而提出的）要求
client	n.	委託人；（律師等的）當事人
commission	n.	佣金
commitment	n.	託付；交託
condition	n.	情況；條件
conditional	a.	附有條件的；以……為條件的
confidential	a.	祕密的；機密的
consent	v.	同意；贊成
content	a.	滿足的；滿意的
contract	n.	契約
	v.	締結；訂（約）
cooperate	v.	合作；協作
correction	n.	訂正；修改
counselor	n.	顧問；律師
counterpart	n.	副本
countersignature	n.	副署；會簽
curtail	v.	縮減；削減
deal	n.	交易
decide	v.	決定
declare	v.	宣布；宣告

deduct	v.	扣除;減除
detail	n.	細節;詳情
discussion	n.	討論;商討
document	n.	公文;文件
draft	n.	草稿;草圖
drawback	n.	缺點;短處
due	a.	應支付的;欠款的
duplicate	a.	完全一樣的;複製的
duration	n.	期間
expire	v.	滿期;屆期
extra	a.	額外的;外加的
government	n.	政府
impose	v.	徵(稅);加(負擔等)於
lawyer	n.	律師;法學家
legal	a.	法律上的
manuscript	a.	手寫的;原稿的
marriage	n.	結婚;婚姻
negotiate	v.	談判;協商
obligation	n.	義務;責任
offer	v.	給予;提供
on behalf of	—	代表
partner	n.	夥伴
partnership	n.	合夥 / 合作關係
penalty	n.	處罰;刑罰
photocopy	v.	影印;複印
private	a.	個人的;私人的
promise	n.	承諾;諾言
property	n.	財產;資產
reconsider	v.	重新考慮
remit	v.	豁免(稅捐等)
renew	v.	使更新;使復原
represent	v.	代表;象徵

revise	v.	修訂;校訂
rise	v.	上升;升起
sign	v.	簽名
signature	n.	簽名
stress	n.	壓力;緊張
stressful	a.	緊張的;壓力大的
submit	v.	提交;建議
tariff	n.	關稅;稅率
tax	n.	稅;稅金
tax authority	—	稅務機關
tax revenue	—	稅收收入
term	n.	期;期限;(契約等的)條件、條款
violation	n.	違反;違背

翻譯

Translation

★ 以下內容與英文不見得字字對應，本書所列出的是最符合語感和情境的翻譯。

Chapter. 1

P. 25 表格

1. 公寓／房屋出租	6. 不動產——自售	10. 我要租房間
2. 我要租公寓	7. 不動產——仲介	11. 短期轉租
3. 短期換屋	8. 我要買房子	12. 我要找短期轉租
4. 商辦	9. 房間分租	13. 假期出租
5. 車位和倉庫		

P. 26 對話

Paul: Carrie，我聽說妳要去遊學。處理得怎樣了？申請宿舍了嗎？

Carrie: 沒，我另有打算。你知道我住宿四年了，這次我想要試著自己一個人生活。

Paul: 那妳找房子一事進行得如何了？有看到什麼喜歡的嗎？

Carrie: 唉，並沒有。我還陷在這些公寓型式的稱謂上呢！張貼廣告內都打上不同的名稱，把我搞混了。

Paul: 別擔心，這我想我可以幫得上妳。

Carrie: 太棒了！從哪開始好呢？（下拉網頁）好，什麼是 studio apartment？

Paul: Studio？這基本上是一間臥房、客廳和小廚房全都連在一起的開放式小套房，另有一全套衛浴。有些人也稱作經濟套房或是單身套房。

Carrie: 那什麼是 one-bedroom apartment？我看到還有 two-bedroom apartment 或 three-bedroom apartment。

Paul: 類似 studio，one-bedroom apartment 也有客廳、廚房、全套衛浴，但臥房是獨立的，所以若有朋友來訪，妳比較有隱私。

Carrie: 那我猜 two-bedroom apartment 應該就有兩間獨立臥房囉？

Paul: 妳答對了！有時還會再多加一間衛浴呢。

Carrie: 啊，我想我現在有漸漸進入狀況了。好，接著要問的是 lofts。

Paul: Loft apartment 是指一個大型的開放空間，具有高天花板且沒有內牆。上層樓通常是睡覺區。

Carrie: 了解。最後一個，penthouse apartment 呢？

Paul: 哇，這妳可能負擔不起。Penthouse apartment 為蓋在頂樓上的特殊建築，裡面什麼都有，被視為豪宅，且無庸置疑地貴。

Carrie: 放心啦，我當然不可能選這個。

P. 32 廣告

> 張貼時間：2016-01-11, 3:13PM
>
> **$2,000 / 2br – 寬敞兩房兩衛公寓 – 隨時入住 (N. Vermont Ave, Hollywood, CA 90033)**
>
> 在 Pleasant Apartment Homes 找尋您奢華的住所吧！ Pleasant 提供寬敞且舒適的兩層樓公寓，內有兩間臥房、兩套全衛、冷暖氣、大型更衣室、私人陽台、四間 24 小時開放的現代化洗衣房，以及固定車位和車庫。
>
> 鄰近購物、娛樂、餐飲，以及 LA 市區。Pleasant 座落於 66 號和 5 號公路附近。可立即入住，約期一年，月租 $2,000 美金，押金 $1,500。
>
> 快來參觀看看吧。我們親切的駐點人員會回答您所有的問題。一週七天隨時歡迎來訪。

P. 38 TOEIC Test

Script

A. 微波爐在烤箱上方。

B. 火爐正被使用中。

C. 不鏽鋼壺掛在牆上。

D. 冰箱是空的。

Chapter.2

P. 41 對話

Paul: 什麼！Carrie 妳還在這？妳到底上網找多久啦？一兩個小時了吧？

Carrie: 事實上，是三個小時了。

Paul: 無法置信！那妳應該找到要的資料了吧。

Carrie: 老實說，並沒有。我迷失在這堆資訊中了。這上面有太多合適的選項，我怎麼有可能全部都瀏覽過？

Paul: 妳沒先排出優先次序嗎？

Carrie: 什麼意思？什麼優先次序？

Paul: 在妳開始搜尋前，妳得先坐下來，列出妳希望這房子該有的東西，像是哪些設施、房屋特徵或租金等。之後選出最重要的前五項，這樣妳才不會陷入一團混亂裡。

Carrie: 好建議。Paul，我真該早點問你的。

Paul: 妳的確應該，看看妳浪費了多少時間！喔，用妳列出來的優先順序幫助挑選。

Carrie: 好的，那開始列清單囉！

Paul: 需要幫忙嗎？

翻譯

P. 42 對話

Carrie: 好的，那開始列清單囉！

Paul: 需要幫忙嗎？

Carrie: 當然好！

Paul: 好，那就讓我們一個一個進行。第一件，先想出五個妳最重視的需求。

Carrie: 嗯……我想是租金低、地點便利、附空調、洗衣機和網路。

Paul: 很好，現在將這五項排序吧。

Carrie: 第一個當然是租金低。你知道我的學費有多貴的，我可負擔不起一個月超過 $950 的公寓。

Paul: 很合理。

Carrie: 第二個是……網路。這個時代沒有網路很難生活啊。

Paul: 確實。我根本無法想像生命中沒有 Google。下一個是什麼？

Carrie: 洗衣機。我不想走得老遠去洗衣服，尤其我還得在那等一個小時後再把衣服帶回來。

Paul: 聽起來妳比較偏好屋內附有洗衣機。那若是附洗衣房設施的呢？

Carrie: 雖可以接受，但不會是我的首選。

Paul: 接著是第四項。

Carrie: 我選地點便利吧，得離學校近的。既然我沒打算買車，走路到學校的距離就不能超過 30 分鐘。

Paul: 我想，這大約是 2 英里吧。所以最後一個是空調囉？

Carrie: 沒錯。聽說 LA 夏天可能比台灣還熱呢！

P. 53 TOEIC Test

Script

對你而言，哪些家用設備是必須的？

參考答案

因為 LA 夏季非常熱，冷氣在我家就扮演了重要角色。此外，洗衣機和烘乾機比手洗省下我許多時間，因此，這兩者也是必要的。但若我只被允許擁有一樣設備，我會選擇高速網路。從學校課業到日常生活，處處都要用到網路。沒網路，就沒生活。

Chapter.3

P. 56 廣告

$700 低價大公寓！快來！

出租資訊

出租價格：$700 ／月

地點：3101 E Artesia Blvd Long Beach, CA 90805

出租單位：套房｜平方英尺：360 英尺｜租約期：12 個月

設備清單

社區

- 加蓋式車位　　　- 駐點管理　　　- 分配車位

單位特色

- 負擔部分公共設施費用　　　- 掛壁式冷氣

- 淋浴間拉門　　- 天花板吊扇　　- 地毯

其他資訊

租賃公司聯繫方式：

www.apts123.net/rent.aspx?p=5C7cyQSu6ck%3d

Artesia 公寓：(562) 506-1929

P. 61 對話

Carrie: 嗨，我是 Carrie，我想和房東約下週看屋。

Landlord: 嗨，我是房東 Jay，我確認一下我的行事曆……下週……我週二和週五有空。妳哪天想來看屋？

Carrie: 嗯……我想約週二，21 號。

Landlord: 好的，妳可以下午來嗎？

Carrie: 喔抱歉，我週二下午不行，可以改週二早上嗎？

Landlord: 好，早上也可以。

Carrie: 太好了，早上十點好嗎？

Landlord: 好的，可以請妳帶妳的身分證件一起過來嗎？

Carrie: 當然。還需要其他的嗎？

Landlord: 不需要，這樣就好。妳知道怎麼來嗎？

Carrie: 不知道，可以跟我說怎麼走嗎？

Landlord: 妳有 email 信箱嗎？我可以把資訊寄給妳。

翻譯

Carrie:	有，你有筆和紙嗎？
Landlord:	有的，請說。
Carrie:	信箱是 abcd123@gmail.com。
Landlord:	好，讓我重複一遍確認一下，信箱是 abcd123@gmail.com。
Carrie:	沒錯，期待你的來信。再見。
Landlord:	再見。

P. 69 TOEIC Test

參考答案

此套房的格局設計良好。

Chapter.4

P. 76 車資說明

Metro 基本費為 $1.5。您可於每次搭乘 Metro 公車時付現（公車駕駛不會準備零錢，因此您需要備妥足額的車資），或是於 Metro Rail 或 Metro 橘線公車各站的 TAP 販賣機，購買可重複使用的 TAP 卡並加值。

持有有效身分證明之年長和行動不便者，可享折扣現金價。

> 溫馨提示：每位付費的成年人可攜帶兩名五歲以下的兒童免費搭乘公車或捷運。

若是您將成為頻繁通勤者，月票或週票可能對您最划算。對學生、年長者和行動不便者，我們提供許多種類的折扣票卡。您也可購買當日票。以上皆為儲值型式之票卡（或稱 TAP 卡），販售於全國數百個地點。

> 溫馨提示：若您使用預付通行證或是 TAP 卡搭乘 Metro 公車，上車時簡單地對著收費箱上的 TAP 標靶輕擊一下；搭乘 Metro Rail 各線和 Metro 橘線公車時，請於進入車站時，在旋轉式票閘處或站內驗票機上輕擊您的票卡。

P. 78 對話

| Carrie: | 不好意思，我在找這個公車站：LAX City Bus Center 搭乘 Metro Local Line 232 路公車，你知道在哪嗎？ |
| Passerby: | 喔，離這不遠，妳沿著 W Century Blvd 走，然後右轉 Airport Dr。 |

Carrie: 右轉 Airport Dr 嗎？好的。

Passerby: 然後繼續沿著 Airport Dr 走兩個路口到 W 96th St。

Carrie: 這樣大約要走多久？

Passerby: 大約 300 碼，差不多四到五分鐘吧！

Carrie: 了解，接著呢？

Passerby: 然後在 W 96th St 左轉。妳會看到公車站在妳右手邊。

Carrie: 太棒了，聽起來很簡單。

Passerby: 確實不難。不用擔心，妳不會錯過的。

Carrie: 謝謝你。

Passerby: 不用客氣。

P. 79 對話

Carrie: 不好意思，請問你住這附近嗎？

Passerby: 是的。

Carrie: 太好了，我正在找這個地址：227 Olive Ave。你可以告訴我怎麼去嗎？

Passerby: 227 Olive Ave？喔，我知道在哪。沿著 E Broadway 走，然後右轉 Olive Ave。

Carrie: 右轉，之後呢？

Passerby: 然後沿著 Olive Ave 走，大約一個路口就到了。

Carrie: 哇，聽起來很近呢。

Passerby: 確實很近，我想大約才 300 碼。

Carrie: 看來我應該不會迷路，謝謝！

Passerby: 不用客氣。

P. 88 TOEIC Test

Script

不好意思，我在找故宮博物院。

A. 抱歉，我不知道歷史博物館在哪裡。

B. 在交叉路口左轉後你就會看到了。

C. 你可以告訴我怎麼去那裡嗎？

Chapter.5

P. 90 表格

Inside / Internal 室內	Yes	No	Note 備註
Is it clean or freshly painted? 房屋是否乾淨或有重新粉刷？			
Are there signs of damp or flaking paint? 是否有受潮的痕跡或掉漆？			
Is there any sign of loose wires? 是否有脫落的電線？			
Are there any water leaks under the sink or in the ceiling? 水槽下和天花板是否有漏水？			
Is the carpet or floor covering in good shape? 地毯或地板的狀態是否良好？			
Are there enough electrical outlets? Do they all work? 有足夠的插座嗎？是否都可以用？			
Is there central heating and central air-conditioning? Do they work properly? 有中央空調嗎？是否能適當運作？			
Do the lights work? 燈是否會亮？			
Do the windows open and close properly? 窗戶是否能適當地開關？			
Are there secure locks on the doors? 門上是否有安全鎖？			
Are smoke alarms fitted? 是否有安裝煙霧警報器？			
Are kitchen appliances such as dishwashers / stove clean and in working order? 廚房設備如洗碗機、爐子等是否乾淨且堪用？			
Turn on the taps. Is the water pressure strong or weak? 打開水龍頭。水壓強或弱？			
Does the hot water service work? 熱水供應是否良好？			
Look under the sink and around cracks. Are there any signs of roaches or rats? 水槽下和裂縫周圍是否有蟑螂或老鼠的蹤跡？			

Do repairs need to be carried out? Are there any broken items of furniture? 是否需要維修？是否有傢俱破損？		
Are there enough closets and are they large enough? 衣櫃是否夠多且夠大？		
Are there curtains? 是否有窗簾？		
Do the bathroom fixtures work? 浴室設備是否可用？		
Are there any leaks? 是否有漏水情形？		
Does the shower work properly? 淋浴設備是否能適當運作？		
Am I allowed to change the decoration like painting in the house? 可否允許改變屋內裝潢如油漆？		

P. 94 對話

Alex: 嗨，Carrie，我聽說妳要搬到 LA，一切還好嗎？

Carrie: 嗨，Alex，真高興接到你電話。事實上我還在找住的地方呢。我已經聯繫了幾位屋主，也安排好了明天要去看第一間房。

Alex: 聽起來很順利，有我可以幫忙的地方嗎？

Carrie: 嗯，既然你問了，我確實是有個問題……

Alex: 快說吧！

Carrie: 好吧。我知道看屋時得檢查屋況，但是我只有屋內的檢查清單，屋外環境該怎麼確認呢？

Alex: 別擔心，妳問對人啦！我可以分享我之前的經驗。

Carrie: 太棒啦！你真是我的英雄啊！

Alex: 好，讓我先去拿我的清單，再把該檢查的問題告訴妳吧。

P. 94 表格

Outside / External 室外	Yes	No	Note 備註
Where do you pick up your mail? Are there individual mailboxes? 你要在哪收信？是否有獨立信箱？			
Has the house ever been burgled? 房屋是否曾經遭竊？			

翻譯

221

Is there too much street noise or noise from nearby apartments? 街道或鄰近住家是否會太吵？			
Is the house near public transport, a school or under a flight path? 距大眾運輸、學校近嗎？或是位於航線下？			
Is there a place to shop for food or groceries nearby? 是否有可以購買食物或日用品的地方？			
Is the neighborhood safe and clean? Will you feel comfortable walking home alone at night? 鄰近地區是否安全乾淨？你放心晚上自己走回家嗎？			
What are the neighbors like? 鄰居如何？			

P. 97 合約內容

租賃契約

1. 當事人　　本協議當事人為
   房東：
   姓名：Edward Murray　　地址：213 Olive Ave
   市／州／郵遞區號：Long Beach, CA 90802　　電話# 562-996-3521
   房客：
   姓名：Carrie Lee　　地址：No. 26, Yongkang St., Da'an Dist.
   市／州／郵遞區號：Taipei City 106, Taiwan (R.O.C.)　　電話# 562-724-8986

2. 物產　　房東出租一套房予房客，套房位於：
   地址：213 Olive Ave　　市／州／郵遞區號：Long Beach, CA 90802

3. 租賃期應始於：2016/03/01 到 2017/02/28

4. 房客須於每月 1 日預先繳交 $850 ／月的房租。

5. 下列設備和傢俱：
   爐子、烤箱、冰箱、洗碗機、洗衣機、烘乾機、冷氣、暖氣、兩個衣櫥、電視、床隨同該物件一起出租。

6. 保證金：履行該契約，房客須存放 $1,700 予房東，作為於租賃期間內對該物件所造成的損害賠償保證。

7. 下列為雙方須分別負擔的公共設施費用：

	房東	房客
電費		✔
瓦斯費	✔	
暖氣和熱水費		✔
水費和污水處理費	✔	
電話費		✔
網路費	✔	
有線電視費	✔	
垃圾回收費	✔	

8. 雙方——以下簽約者——同意此租賃契約

房東	房客
Edward Murray	Carrie Lee
02/10/2016	02/10/2016

P. 99 對話

Edward: 妳覺得這間套房怎麼樣？

Carrie: 很棒，我非常喜歡。

Edward: 這房子都 OK 嗎？妳都沒有問題嗎？

Carrie: 事實上，我確實有幾個問題。

Edward: 是什麼呢？

Carrie: 左邊牆上有些掉漆。

Edward: 別擔心，妳搬進來前我會重新粉刷過。

Carrie: 是嗎？

Edward: 我一定會。除了這之外，還有什麼問題嗎？

Carrie: 我還注意到電視壞了。

Edward: 喔，我已經買了一台新的，下週一就會送到了。

Carrie: 太棒了，好吧，我想我要租這。

Edward: 真高興聽到妳這麼說。

Carrie: 租金是多少呢？

Edward: 一個月 950 元。

Carrie: 這有點多。

Edward: 我認為很合理。

Carrie: 那水電雜費都包含了嗎？

Edward: 沒有喔，妳得要付電費、暖氣熱水和電話費。

Carrie: 哇，這樣我一個月可能得付超過 1,000 元了。我想我付不起。

Edward: 那妳能付多少呢？

Carrie: 850 元可以嗎？我有查過這附近的價格，如果我要負擔部分的水電雜費，我想這個價格應該很合理。

Edward: 嗯……我得想想。

Carrie: 你看過我先前的租屋紀錄，我都是準時交租，也沒製造過任何問題或是違反規定，你可以再考慮一下我的提議嗎？

Edward: 這倒是沒錯，好吧，我想我可以勉強接受啦！

Carrie: 太棒了，那就這樣說定啦！

P. 106 TOEIC Test

出租物產維修責任

當屋子需要維修時，你可能沒有時間和你的房東或房客爭論維修費用，但你肯定不會想要負擔不屬於你責任的部分。因此，了解相互的權利和責任是減少爭議費用和時間的最好方式。

基本上，如果是出於長時間損耗所造成的維修，房東須負擔該費用。但是若毀損是出於人為的結果，則應該由房客負擔維修費。舉例來說，當水龍頭因為長時間的腐蝕而破裂，房東應負責維修。另一方面，若是由於某種錯誤操作產生的破裂，則房客應負擔該損失。

Q1.

這篇文章主要關於什麼？

(A) 屋主的責任

(B) 承包商的責任

(C) 出租人和居住者的責任

(D) 房仲的責任

Q2.

最有可能在哪裡看到這篇文章？

(A) 房屋修繕雜誌

(B) 報紙廣告

(C) 居家維修店

(D) 租屋規範指南

Chapter.6

P. 109 帳戶介紹

活期戶：活期戶讓您簡易取得存款，作為平日交易使用，並為您安全保管現金。客戶可使用現金卡、支票購物或者支付帳單。帳戶提供不同選擇或組合，幫助您免除某些月費。

儲蓄戶：儲蓄戶讓您能從您所儲蓄的資金中累積利息。利率可以日、週、月或以年為基準複算。根據月費、利率、計算利率方式，以及開戶存款額，儲蓄戶可有不同的選擇。

P. 112 對話

Bank teller: 早安，有什麼我可以為您服務的？

Carrie: 我想開戶。

Bank teller: 好的，您想開哪種戶呢？活期戶還是儲蓄戶？

Carrie: 這兩種差異在哪？

Bank teller: 您能輕易運用活期戶裡的金錢，也就是說，您隨時都可以提領。但是活期戶沒有給付利息。至於儲蓄戶，目前一年的定期利率是 2.35%，三年則是 3.5%。不過您一個月從儲蓄戶提領的次數不能超過六次。

Carrie: 喔，我了解了。嗯……我只是來唸書的，我想我還是選擇開活期戶好了。

Bank teller: 沒問題，您今天想要存多少進帳戶呢？我們開戶的最低金額是 $50。

Carrie: 我要存 $3,000。

Bank teller: 好的，請填寫這張表格並給我您的護照和學生證，我立即為您開戶。

P. 122 TOEIC Test

Script

我想開一個活期存款帳戶。

A. 你可以在這裡報到。

B. 你的帳號號碼是？

C. 請先填寫這些表格。

225

P. 127 對話

Server: 午安您好，我是您今天的侍者，要喝點什麼嗎？

Carrie: 請給我一杯柳橙汁加冰。

Server: 好的，我馬上回來。

·····（3 分鐘後）·····

Server: 這是您的柳橙汁。您準備好要點餐了嗎？還是需要再等一下？

Carrie: 我準備好了。我想先來個奶油蟹肉餅和巧達湯。

Server: 很棒的選擇。那您的主菜想要什麼呢？

Carrie: 我還不太確定，這裡有什麼好吃的嗎？

Server: 我推薦您試試肋眼牛排，這非常受歡迎。

Carrie: 好，那我就點肋眼牛排吧。

Server: 沒問題，您的牛排想要幾分熟呢？

Carrie: 七分，謝謝。

Server: 肋眼牛排有附一道配菜，我們有馬鈴薯泥、烤馬鈴薯或薯條，您想要哪一種呢？

Carrie: 我要薯條。

Server: 好的，所以您點的是一份奶油蟹肉餅、一份巧達湯、一份肋眼牛排加薯條。您的餐點很快就會送來。

·····（1 小時後）·····

Server: 餐點還好嗎？

Carrie: 很美味！我非常喜歡。

Server: 您要來點甜點嗎？

Carrie: 好的，可以給我甜點的菜單嗎？

Server: 菜單在這。

Carrie: 紅絲絨布朗尼和香蕉布丁看起來都很美味。

Server: 這兩種都很棒。但若是您喜歡甜一點，您可以試試布朗尼。

Carrie: 喔，我沒這麼愛吃甜，我想我試布丁好了。

Server: 沒問題。

小費禮儀

在餐廳用餐，我們應該給多少小費呢？這隨著各種因素而異，像是餐廳的等級、用餐人數、服務種類，以及服務品質。

在美國，小費一般為稅前總消費額的 10 ～ 20%。服務優異給 20%，服務一般的給 15%，而服務不佳則給 10%。

然而，許多餐廳會主動對六人以上的團體收取小費。所以別忘了檢查是否小費已經涵蓋在帳單裡囉！

P. 131 對話

Server: 餐點還好嗎？

Carrie: 很美味，但我很飽了。我想將剩下的帶回去，可以請你給我一個外帶盒嗎？

Server: 別擔心，我會幫您打包好的。

Carrie: 太棒了，謝謝。

P. 135 TOEIC Test

保持恰當的＿＿＿＿＿＿＿＿對於商務會議而言，可促進參與者之間的尊重和合作，幫助會議更具效能和效率。

(A) 適當

(B) 本質；要素

(C) 複雜性

(D) 禮儀

Chapter.8

P. 140 對話

1. 詢問特定顏色或尺寸：

Carrie: 請問，你們這件襯衫有藍色的嗎？

Salesperson: 有的，需要拿給您嗎？

Carrie: 請問，你們這件襯衫有六號嗎？

Salesperson: 有的，我去拿給您。

翻譯

Carrie:	不好意思，這件襯衫可以給我小號的嗎？
Salesperson:	好的，我馬上回來。

2. 詢問不特定尺寸：

Carrie:	請問，你們這件襯衫有小件一點的嗎？
Salesperson:	有的，讓我看看……這件是大號，我去拿中號的給您。

3. 詢問不特定顏色：

Carrie:	請問，這件襯衫有其他顏色嗎？
Salesperson:	有的，這有三個顏色，藍色、灰色和白色。

....

Carrie:	請問，這件襯衫有其他顏色嗎？
Salesperson:	有的，我們還有藍色、灰色和白色。

P. 141 對話

1. 在店內（尋找更衣間）：

Carrie:	你好，我可以在哪試穿呢？
Salesperson:	更衣間在那邊。

....（3 分鐘後）...

Salesperson:	穿起來怎樣？
Carrie:	很好，我要了。

2. 在更衣間（件數限制）：

Carrie:	嗨，我想試穿。
Salesperson:	好的，您有多少件呢？
Carrie:	嗯……六件。
Salesperson:	（開門）請進，若有需要其他尺寸的話請告知我。

....（10 分鐘後）...

Salesperson:	有適合的嗎？
Carrie:	並沒有，都不太適合我。

3. 在店內（店員主動接近）：

Salesperson:	嗨，找得還順利嗎？需要試穿這件嗎？
Carrie:	是的，麻煩你。
Salesperson:	好的，我幫您拿到更衣間。

....（3 分鐘後）...

Salesperson: 這條裙子您穿起來很可愛。

Carrie: 謝謝。

4. 在店內（店員主動接近）:

Salesperson: 嗨，需要我幫您安排間更衣室嗎？

Carrie: 那太好了。

Salesperson: 您的名字？

Carrie: Carrie。

Salesperson: 好的。

P. 144 短文

Lady House 退換貨規定

如果您不滿意您所購買的商品，您可以在購買日後的三十天內退回或更換。商品必須要是未磨損、洗滌或修改過，且標籤未拆。全國所有的 Lady House 商店都接受退貨。

商品必須附上原收據以便退貨或更換。退回款項會依據原先付款型式退還。支票退款須收取 25 美元的服務費。

購買日後三十天，或是最後折扣的商品不接受退換貨。

P. 146 對話

Salesperson: 嗨，就這些嗎？還有其他需要嗎？

Carrie: 不了，就這樣，謝謝。

Salesperson: 今天購物有人幫您嗎？

Carrie: 有的，我想她的名字應該是 Katherine。

Salesperson: 好的。

Carrie: 喔……可以請你幫我確認一下這件的價格有打折嗎？

Salesperson: 我看看……有的，這件打七折。

Carrie: 太好了，謝謝。

Salesperson: 您消費的總金額爲 $ 250.47，您要刷卡還是付現？

Carrie: 你們收旅行支票嗎？

Salesperson: 不好意思，我們不收任何種類的支票。

Carrie: 沒關係，我刷卡好了。喔……糟了！我把卡留在家了。好吧，看來我只能付現了。

Salesperson: 這是找您的錢。收據要放在袋內還是給您？

Carrie: 放在袋內。順便問一下，你們接受退貨嗎？

翻譯

229

Salesperson: 接受。我們的退貨規定就印在收據上。

Carrie: 謝謝。

Salesperson: 不客氣，祝您有個美好的一天。

P. 151 TOEIC Test

退貨規定
無退款

只接受換貨

原狀退回之商品可於購買後 45 天內，攜帶原收據，更換其他商品或兌換店內消費點數。

更多退貨規定資訊，請上我們的網站 www.happyshopping.com。此外，我們銷售服務人員將會很樂意於電話上回應您的任何問題。

聯絡電話：810-337-5911

如要換貨須攜帶什麼？

(A) 原商品和購買收據

(B) 原商品和信用卡

(C) 購買收據和信用卡

(D) 額外現金和原包裝

Chapter.9

P. 156 對話

Carrie: 你在家啊，謝天謝地！

Steven: 怎麼了嗎？

Carrie: 喔，我正打算寄個禮物回台灣。但是我從沒寄過國際郵件，想先知道一下價錢。

Steven: 妳確實需要，國際郵件通常很貴的。妳需要網址嗎？我可以幫妳找。

Carrie: 其實，我正卡在那個網頁上。

Steven: 怎麼會？不是只要把資訊填入空格就好了嗎？

Carrie: 問題是我不知道這些空格是在問什麼。你可以過來幫幫我嗎？

Steven: 好，讓我瞧瞧……選擇目的地，這個妳只要選擇要寄達的地方即可，台灣對吧？

Carrie: 對。

Steven: 然後輸入禮物的價格。

Carrie: 禮物？ 120 美元。這兒的寄件日期是填今天對吧？

Steven: 沒錯！

Carrie: 好，我猜下一步是要選適合的包裝。但這個 flat rate 是什麼意思？

Steven: 這表示針對同一種尺寸的包裝，不論物品的重量，只要妳塞得進去，都只算一個價格。等等……每種包裝是有限重的，所以注意妳的禮物別超過了。

Carrie: 懂了，謝啦！

P. 163 郵寄服務介紹

Global Express Guaranteed® （全球快遞）
一到三個工作天
Global Express Guaranteed® (GXG®) 為我們最快的國際郵寄服務。具競爭力的國際郵寄費率、明確寄達日及保證退款，服務範圍超過 180 國。運送服務由 FedEx Express 公司提供。$55.85 起。

Priority Mail Express International® （國際限時郵件）
三到五個工作天
提供超過 180 個國家合理且快速的國際郵寄服務，部分國家保證退款。單一國際郵寄價格且提供免費包裝耗材。線上購買可享零售價的折扣。$38.00 起。

Priority Mail International® （國際快捷郵件）
六到十個工作天
提供超過 180 個國家可靠且合理的郵寄服務。此外，線上購買可享單一國際郵寄價格、免費包裝耗材及零售價的折扣優惠。$37.50 起。

P. 164 郵寄服務介紹

First-Class Mail International® （一般國際郵件）
價格合理的國際郵件服務
郵寄明信片、信封或大型信件最划算的選擇。寄送超過 180 個國家，最重可達四磅（價值不超過 $400）。郵局售價 $1.20 起。

First-Class Package International Service® （一般國際包裹）
價格合理的國際郵件服務
寄送小型包裹最經濟的方式。服務超過 180 個國家，最重可達四磅（價值不超過 $400）。郵局售價 $7.10 起。

翻譯

231

Script

嗨，我想寄這件包裹到台灣。

A. 這是誰的信？

B. 這被包裝在一個小箱子裡。

C. 您想怎麼寄送呢？

Chapter.10

P. 180 對話

Operator: T-Mobile 您好，有什麼我可以為您服務的嗎？

Carrie: 您好，我想要申辦手機通話方案。

Operator: 沒問題，您想要申辦哪個方案呢？

Carrie: 其實我有上你們網站查過了，我對月租 50 美元的預付卡方案非常感興趣。但我不確定我是否得簽約。

Operator: T-Mobile 的所有通話方案都不再需要綁約了。

Carrie: 太好了！那流量超額怎麼計算？我看到這個方案可以使用 4G 寬頻 2GB 的流量，那若是我超過這個數量，得付多少呢？

Operator: 我們不收取任何的國內超額費用。也就是說，若是您超出了所給予的流量數，您仍舊可以繼續使用，只是速度會減緩。除了相關的稅和附加費，您需要負擔的只會有 50 元。

Carrie: 棒呆了！那我就申辦這個方案吧。我該怎麼做？

Operator: 您要購買新機或是使用您自己的呢？

Carrie: 我不需要新機，我自己有 iPhone。

Operator: 這樣的話就簡單多了！連上我們 T-Mobile 的網站，在上方的 SHOP 裡點選 BRING YOUR OWN DEVICE。現在您會看到三個步驟。第一，先確認您的手機是否和我們的網路相容，若沒有問題，您就可以在第二步驟裡購買 SIM 卡了。

P. 190 TOEIC Test

Script

嗨，我想下個月取消我目前的電話服務。需要付中止費嗎？

A. 好的，我們下個月會中止您的通話。

B. 需要，因為這是一年合約，您必須付 200 元。

C. 我欠你多少錢？

〔第一章 P. 24, 25 網頁擷圖〕craigslist　http://losangeles.craigslist.org/hhh

〔第 28 頁〕

圖 1 左：New York Habitat　http://www.nyhabitat.com/new-york-apartment/furnished/16710

圖 1 右：New York Habitat　http://www.nyhabitat.com/new-york-apartment/furnished/16728

圖 2：Magnolia Assisted Living, LLC.　http://www.magnoliaseniorliving.com/floorplans.php

〔第 29 頁〕

圖 3：17 Chapel, L.L.C.　http://www.albanydowntowncondo.com/floorplans.php

圖 4：New York Habitat　http://www.nyhabitat.com/new-york-apartment/furnished/8901

圖 5：貝塔編輯部

〔第 31 頁〕

圖 1, 10：photo AC　www.photo-ac.com

圖 2, 3, 4, 5, 7, 8, 9：作者蕭婉珍

圖 6：貝塔編輯部

〔第 33 頁〕photo AC　www.photo-ac.com

〔第 38 頁〕Wikimedia Commons　https://commons.wikimedia.org/wiki/File:Newly_renovated_
kitchen_with_cabinets_refrigerator_stove_and_hardwood_floor.jpg

〔第二章 P. 46 網頁擷圖〕Google Maps

上：https://www.google.com.tw/maps/place/227+Olive+Ave,+Long+Beach,+CA+90802%E7%B
E%8E%E5%9C%8B/@33.7699154,-118.1849557,17z/data=!3m1!4b1!4m2!3m1!1s0x80dd313df
e61077b:0x60960a2018b5e3d4?hl=zh-TW

下：https://www.google.com.tw/maps/place/227+Olive+Ave,+Long+Beach,+CA+90802%E7%B
E%8E%E5%9C%8B/@33.769919,-118.1824031,3a,75y,268h,90t/data=!3m7!1e1!3m5!1shKJgul
Y13X7c3WXvamjl8Q!2e0!6s%2F%2Fgeo3.ggpht.com%2Fcbk%3Fpanoid%3DhKJgulY13X7c3
WXvamjl8Q%26output%3Dthumbnail%26cb_client%3Dsearch.TACTILE.gps%26thumb%3D2
%26w%3D392%26h%3D106%26yaw%3D268.47159%26pitch%3D0!7i13312!8i6656!4m2!3m1
!1s0x80dd313dfe61077b:0x60960a2018b5e3d4!6m1!1e1?hl=zh-TW

〔P. 47 網頁擷圖〕Google Maps　https://www.google.com.tw/maps/dir/227+Olive+Ave,+Long+
Beach,+CA+90802%E7%BE%8E%E5%9C%8B/Long+Beach+City+College-Aviation+Departm
ent,+East+Pacific+Coast+Highway,+%E9%95%B7%E7%81%98%E5%8A%A0%E5%88%A9%
E7%A6%8F%E5%B0%BC%E4%BA%9E%E5%B7%9E%E7%BE%8E%E5%9C%8B/@33.780
2119,-118.1871239,15z/data=!3m1!4b1!4m14!4m13!1m5!1m1!1s0x80dd313dfe61077b:0x60960
a2018b5e3d4!2m2!1d-118.182767!2d33.769911!1m5!1m1!1s0x80dd3164338073b7:0x505723ed
1fa74671!2m2!1d-118.1739719!2d33.7904782!3e2?hl=zh-TW

〔第 44, 45 頁〕Apt 1, 2, 3 示意圖：SILHOUETTE AC　www.silhouette-ac.com

〔第 47 頁〕下方情境圖：photo AC　www.photo-ac.com

〔第 59 頁〕下方情境圖：photo AC　www.photo-ac.com

〔第 69 頁〕photo AC　www.photo-ac.com

〔第四章 P. 72, 73（上）網頁擷圖〕LA Metro　www.metro.net

〔P. 73（下）, 74, 75 網頁擷圖〕LA Metro　https://trips.metro.net/tm_pub_start.php?place0=LAX+CITY+BUS+CENTER&place1=227+Olive+Ave%2C+Long+Beach%2C+CA+90802&timecrit0=AR&day0=MON&hour0=+10&min0=+02&ampm0=P&fare=RG&evaluateButton=+Plan+My+Trip

〔P. 79 網頁擷圖〕Google Maps　https://www.google.com.tw/maps/dir/LAX+Lot+C+Bus+Terminal,+W+96th+St,+Los+Angeles,+CA+90045/Los+Angeles+Airport+Marriott,+West+Century+Boulevard,+Los+Angeles,+CA,+United+States/@33.9473895,-118.3904439,17z/data=!3m1!4b1!4m14!4m13!1m5!1m1!1s0x80c2b6d55f5bcbbd:0x221e489cb235c893!2m2!1d-118.3917894!2d33.9491907!1m5!1m1!1s0x80c2b6d6d68ea5ff:0x648380118851f3ae!2m2!1d-118.3848086!2d33.9465953!3e2

〔P. 80 網頁擷圖〕Google Maps　https://www.google.com.tw/maps/dir/E+Broadway+%26+Alamitos+Ave,+Long+Beach,+CA+90802%E7%BE%8E%E5%9C%8B/227+N+Olive+Ave,+Long+Beach,+CA+90802%E7%BE%8E%E5%9C%8B/@33.7694611,-118.1827331,19.25z/am=t/data=!4m14!4m13!1m5!1m1!1s0x80dd3116192e3001:0x4483f7cb50ce2b95!2m2!1d-118.1820822!2d33.7691442!1m5!1m1!1s0x80dd3115ffe145df:0xd69beaa90c397b84!2m2!1d-118.1824031!2d33.7699318!3e2

〔第 92 頁〕

圖 1, 2, 3, 6, 7, 8, 9, 10, 12：photo AC　www.photo-ac.com

圖 4：Kansei.co.Ldt.　http://kansei-zosan.co.jp/blog/2012/08/27/1105

圖 5, 13, 14, 15：作者蕭婉珍

圖 11：EnviroVent Ltd　www.envirovent.com/home-ventilation/find-a-local-damp-surveyor/

〔第五章 P. 96 網頁擷圖〕Rentometer　www.rentometer.com

〔P. 101 網頁擷圖〕Rentometer　https://www.rentometer.com/results/CdQK_E8I0jA

〔第 105 頁〕下方情境圖：作者蕭婉珍

〔第 110 頁〕旅行支票樣本圖：台灣美國運通國際股份有限公司　http://www.americanexpress.com/taiwan/tc/learn-more.shtml

〔第 113 頁〕下方情境圖：photo AC　www.photo-ac.com

〔第 125 頁〕四幅食物圖：photo AC　www.photo-ac.com

〔第 138 頁〕

三幅鞋子圖：Illust AC　www.ac-illust.com

廣告底圖：photo AC　www.photo-ac.com

〔第 143 頁〕右上情境圖：作者蕭婉珍

〔第 145 頁〕下方情境圖：作者蕭婉珍

〔第九章 P. 154 網頁擷圖〕USPS　www.usps.com

〔P. 155 網頁擷圖〕https://www.usps.com/international/welcome.htm

〔P. 156, 159 網頁擷圖〕https://ircalc.usps.com/

〔P. 163 網頁擷圖〕https://www.usps.com/international/mail-shipping-services.htm

〔第 157 頁〕中間情境圖：photo AC　www.photo-ac.com

〔第 159 頁〕兩幅郵件包裝圖：作者蕭婉珍

〔第 165 頁〕

圖 A：Wallpaper Craft　https://wallpaperscraft.com/wallpaper/weapon_pistol_ammunition_metal_44488

圖 B, C, D, F, G, J：photo AC　www.photo-ac.com

圖 E：貝塔編輯部

圖 H：ICOON MONO　http://icooon-mono.com/en/15814-poison-icon

圖 I：Icon-rainbow　http://free-icon-rainbow.com/hair-spray-free-icon-3/

〔第 166, 167 頁〕郵寄報關單圖：https://jenschwab.wordpress.com/2010/11/23/how-a-package-gets-to-the-sandbox/

更多表單最新資料：USPS　http://about.usps.com/forms/ps2976a.pdf

〔第十章 P. 176 網頁擷圖〕T-Mobile　www.t-mobile.com

〔P. 178 網頁擷圖〕http://prepaid-phones.t-mobile.com/prepaid-plans

〔P. 179 網頁擷圖〕http://prepaid-phones.t-mobile.com/simple-choice-prepaid-plans

〔P. 182 網頁擷圖〕

上：http://prepaid-phones.t-mobile.com/other-prepaid-plans

下：http://prepaid-phones.t-mobile.com/prepaid-monthly-plans?icid=WMM_PD_SMPLYPRPD1_0AKDHJ8FRJ3752

〔P. 183 網頁擷圖〕http://prepaid-phones.t-mobile.com/pay-as-you-go

〔P. 184 網頁擷圖〕

上：http://prepaid-phones.t-mobile.com/simple-choice-prepaid-plans

下：http://www.t-mobile.com/optional-services/international-calling.html?icid=WMD_PD_STTSDSCNA_8IM5UK10BPB2650#check-rates

〔第 185 頁〕

圖 A：貝塔編輯部

圖 B 電話機：SILHOUETTE AC　www.silhouette-ac.com

圖 C 手機：Illust AC　www.ac-illust.com

下方情境圖：photo AC　www.photo-ac.com

〔P. 186 網頁擷圖〕http://www.t-mobile.com/optional-services/international-calling.html?icid=WMD_PD_STTSDSCNA_8IM5UK10BPB2650#check-rates

國家圖書館出版品預行編目資料

解決問題的英語力 / 陳超明、蕭婉珍作. -- 初版. --
臺北市：貝塔, 2016.03
面；　公分
ISBN 978-986-92044-6-0（平裝附光碟片）

1. 英語　2.讀本

805.18　　　　　　　　　　　　　　　　105001869

解決問題的英語力

作　　者 / 陳超明、蕭婉珍
執行編輯 / 游玉旻
英文協力 / David Katz

出　　版 / 貝塔出版有限公司
地　　址 / 100 台北市館前路 12 號 11 樓
電　　話 / (02)2314-2525
傳　　真 / (02)2312-3535
客服專線 / (02)2314-3535
客服信箱 / btservice@betamedia.com.tw
郵撥帳號 / 19493777
郵撥戶名 / 貝塔出版有限公司

總 經 銷 / 時報文化出版企業股份有限公司
地　　址 / 桃園市龜山區萬壽路二段 351 號
電　　話 / (02)2306-6842

出版日期 / 2016 年 3 月初版一刷
定　　價 / 400 元
海外定價 / 美金 18 元
I S B N / 978-986-92044-6-0

解決問題的英語力
Copyright 2016 by 陳超明、蕭婉珍
Published by Beta Multimedia Publishing

喚醒你的英文語感！

請對折後釘好，直接寄回即可！

100 台北市中正區館前路12號11樓

 貝塔語言出版 收
Beta Multimedia Publishing

寄件者住址 □ □ □

貝塔語言出版
Beta Multimedia Publishing

讀者服務專線（02）2314-3535　　讀者服務傳真（02）2312-3535
客戶服務信箱 btservice@betamedia.com.tw

www.betamedia.com.tw

謝謝您購買本書！！

貝塔語言擁有最優良之英文學習書籍，為提供您最佳的英語學習資訊，您可填妥此表後寄回（免貼郵票）將可不定期收到本公司最新發行書訊及活動訊息！

姓名：_____　性別：□男 □女　生日：_____年_____月_____日

電話：(公)_____(宅)_____(手機)_____

電子信箱：_____

學歷：□高中職含以下 □專科 □大學 □研究所含以上

職業：□金融 □服務 □傳播 □製造 □資訊 □軍公教 □出版
　　　□自由 □教育 □學生 □其他

職級：□企業負責人 □高階主管 □中階主管 □職員 □專業人士

1. 您購買的書籍是？_____

2. 您從何處得知本產品？(可複選)

　　　□書店 □網路 □書展 □校園活動 □廣告信函 □他人推薦 □新聞報導 □其他

3. 您覺得本產品價格：

　　　□偏高 □合理 □偏低

4. 請問目前您每週花了多少時間學英語？

　　　□ 不到十分鐘 □ 十分鐘以上，但不到半小時 □ 半小時以上，但不到一小時

　　　□ 一小時以上，但不到兩小時 □ 兩個小時以上 □ 不一定

5. 通常在選擇語言學習書時，哪些因素是您會考慮的？

　　　□ 封面 □ 內容、實用性 □ 品牌 □ 媒體、朋友推薦 □ 價格□ 其他_____

6. 市面上您最需要的語言書種類為？

　　　□ 聽力 □ 閱讀 □ 文法 □ 口說 □ 寫作 □ 其他_____

7. 通常您會透過何種方式選購語言學習書籍？

　　　□ 書店門市 □ 網路書店 □ 郵購 □ 直接找出版社 □ 學校或公司團購

　　　□ 其他_____

8. 給我們的建議：_____

_____

喚醒你的英文語感！

Get a Feel for English !

喚醒你的英文語感！

Get a Feel for English !